A Note from Stephanie About a Whole New Me

It's the beginning of the seventh grade, and I decided to make some serious changes in my life, starting with myself. You know, like working harder in school and being more responsible at home. It all seemed so simple the night before my first day back to school. But boy, was I in for some surprises.

Before I get ahead of myself, let me introduce my family, because they played a big part in the search for the new Stephanie. You see, the Tanner family isn't an ordinary family. It's a *very* large family.

Right now there are nine people and a dog living in our house—and for all I know, someone new could move in at any time. There's me, my big sister, D.J.; my little sister, Michelle; and my dad, Danny. But that's just the beginning.

Uncle Jesse came first. My dad asked him to come live with us when my mom died, to help take care of me and my sisters.

Back then, Uncle Jesse didn't know much about taking care of three little girls. He was more into rock 'n' roll. So Dad asked his old college buddy, Joey Gladstone, to help out. Joey didn't know anything about kids, either—but it sure was funny watching him learn!

Having Uncle Jesse and Joey around was like having three dads instead of one! But then something even better happened—Uncle Jesse fell in love. He married Becky Donaldson, Dad's co-host on his TV show, *Wake Up, San Francisco*. Aunt Becky's so nice—she's more like a big sister than an aunt.

Next Uncle Jesse and Aunt Becky had twin baby boys. Their names are Nicky and Alex, and they are adorable!

I love being part of a big family. Still, things can get pretty crazy when you live in such a full house!

FULL HOUSE™: Stephanie novels

Phone Call from a Flamingo
The Boy-Oh-Boy Next Door
Twin Troubles
Hip Hop Till You Drop
Here Comes the Brand-New Me
The Secret's Out
Daddy's Not-So-Little Girl
P.S. Friends Forever
Getting Even with the Flamingoes
The Dude of My Dreams

Available from MINSTREL Books

FULL HOUSE™
Stephanie

Here Comes the Brand-New Me

Jacqueline Carroll

A Parachute Press Book

Allie

A
MINSTREL®
BOOK

PUBLISHED BY POCKET BOOKS

New York   London   Toronto   Sydney   Tokyo   Singapore

This book is a work of fiction. Names, characters, places and incidents are products of the author's imagination or are used fictitiously. Any resemblance to actual events or locales or persons, living or dead, is entirely coincidental.

A MINSTREL PAPERBACK *Original*

 A Minstrel Book published by
POCKET BOOKS, a division of Simon & Schuster Inc.
1230 Avenue of the Americas, New York, NY 10020

A Parachute Press Book
Copyright © 1994 by Lorimar Television Inc.

FULL HOUSE, characters, names and all related indicia are trademarks of Lorimar Television © 1994.

ISBN: 0-671-89858-2

First Minstrel Books printing October 1994

10 9 8 7 6 5 4 3

A MINSTREL BOOK and colophon are registered trademarks of Simon & Schuster Inc.

Cover photo by Schultz Photography

Printed in the U.S.A.

Here Comes the Brand-New Me

CHAPTER

1

◆ ◀ ◼ ◆

"Ta-da!" Stephanie Tanner emerged from the dressing room of Lane's department store and turned in front of the full-length mirror. She was wearing a tan cotton sweater over a long white skirt, and a floppy hat with a big white flower in the brim.

"Well?" she asked her two best friends, Allie Taylor and Darcy Powell. "What do you think?"

"Totally cool!" said Allie, brushing her wavy, light-brown hair back from her face.

Darcy, who was tall and slender and looked a little like Whitney Houston, tilted her head to one side and narrowed her eyes critically. Then she smiled. "Awesome!"

1

Stephanie grinned. "Great! Don't move, guys. I'll be out in a second." She dashed back into the dressing room to change into her jeans and T-shirt. When she came out again, she was carrying not only the clothes she'd just tried on, but two pairs of periwinkle tights, some lacy socks, and a shoebox with a pair of Doc Martens in it.

"I just have one question," Darcy said as she and Allie followed Stephanie to the cashier. "Who's paying for all that?"

Stephanie flashed her father's credit card in the air.

"Your dad's plastic!" Darcy exclaimed. "What did you have to do to get that, Steph?

"Nothing. My dad trusts me," Stephanie said as the cashier punched in the prices. "After all, I'm twelve now. I'm more mature. More responsible."

"I'm twelve, too. Why won't *my* dad loan me his credit card?" Darcy asked.

"Probably because he knows you'd charge it to the max," Allie answered.

Stephanie signed the credit card receipt and took the shopping bag from the cashier. "Next stop—jewelry," she announced to her friends.

"Necklaces. Bracelets. Earrings. And barrettes. Silver ones."

"*Silver* barrettes?" Allie's green eyes widened in surprise. "I thought you liked those plastic ones with the pink flowers on them."

"Pink's out," Stephanie declared. "That was the *old* Stephanie. You're looking at the *new* Stephanie."

Allie and Darcy exchanged glances.

"You want to explain this new Stephanie thing to us?" Allie asked as they stopped in front of a glass jewelry counter.

"It's simple," Stephanie replied, spinning one of the necklace displays. "School starts tomorrow, right?"

"Right," Allie agreed. "It's our first day in seventh grade. So you're changing your image with Doc Martens and silver barrettes, is that it?"

"It's not just image; it's a new me," Stephanie said. "And it isn't just new clothes. It's a whole new outlook on life."

"And what exactly does *that* mean?" Darcy asked.

"Well, take school for example." Stephanie moved on to a display of barrettes. "No more daydreaming or doodling on my notebook cov-

3

ers. It's going to be straight A's, even in gym class."

"Straight A's in *gym?*" Darcy said. "You're the one who asked the nurse for permission to get out of volleyball because you broke a fingernail!"

"I'm serious, Darce," Stephanie insisted as she picked out two different silver barrettes. "It's all part of the plan to be more responsible. More together."

Stephanie held one of the barrettes up to her long blond hair. "Like, there'll be no more rushing to get ready for school," she went on. "Starting now I'm going to make my lunch and lay out my clothes the night before." She studied the other barrette. "Which one of these do you like?" she asked.

"Both," Allie said.

As Stephanie was trying to decide between the two barrettes, her younger sister, Michelle, came skipping down the aisle. D.J., Stephanie's older sister, was a few steps behind. Seeing them, Darcy tapped Stephanie on the shoulder. "How's the *new* mature Stephanie going to deal with her *old* little sister?" she asked with a grin.

"I've thought about that, too," Stephanie said as she watched eight-year-old Michelle approach them. "The new me is not going to let Michelle get under my skin. All it takes is patience. Patience and understanding."

"This I gotta see," Allie muttered under her breath.

"Wow, Steph, neat barrettes!" Michelle skidded to a stop next to her sister. "Are you going to buy them?"

"Yes, but I haven't decided which ones." Stephanie winked at Allie and Darcy. She held the barrettes out for Michelle. "What's *your* opinion, Michelle?" she asked seriously.

Michelle grabbed the two mismatched barrettes from Stephanie's hand and examined them. "This one," she said, holding up the one shaped like a silver leaf.

"Really? That's my choice, too." Stephanie held out her hand for the barrettes, but Michelle curled her hands up in tight little fists and wouldn't let go of them. "Since I helped you pick it out, can I wear it sometime?" she asked.

Yeah, and lose it, Stephanie thought to herself.

But how would the new Stephanie react? She'd be much more patient and understanding, Stephanie decided. "Sure, Michelle," she told her sister. "You can wear the barrette some time."

Michelle looked doubtful. "You really mean it?"

"Yes, Michelle, I really mean it."

Michelle smiled and handed over the barrettes. Darcy and Allie flashed her surprised looks.

"Notice I didn't say *when*," Stephanie whispered to her friends as Michelle wandered over to a display of silky lingerie. "Just *some* time."

"I think I'm catching on," Darcy said.

"Hi, guys," D.J. said, joining the group. She looked down at Stephanie's shopping bag. "Whoa! You'd better be careful, Steph, or Dad will have cardiac arrest when he sees his next credit card bill."

"Don't worry, D.J. Most of this stuff was on sale, and I've got just a few more things to buy."

As Stephanie was paying for the barrette, Allie nudged her in the side.

"Don't look now," Allie whispered, "but your little sister is about to test your patience and understanding again."

Turning, Stephanie saw Michelle admiring herself in front of a triple mirror. She was wearing a white lace bra *over* her sweatshirt.

Stephanie could feel her face turning bright red. *Remain calm*, she told herself. *Pretend you don't even know the eight-year-old wearing the woman's bra. Never saw her before in your life.*

"How do I look, Stephanie?" Michelle sang out loudly.

Allie and Darcy giggled. A woman walking down the aisle glanced at Michelle and smiled. The guy at the cash register got a look at Michelle and *didn't* smile.

Trying hard to remain calm, Stephanie said, "I don't think so, Michelle. Maybe in five years. Come on, guys," she added to her friends. "We've got some serious shopping to do. Good luck, D.J."

Still giggling, Allie and Darcy followed a briskly moving Stephanie out of the department store.

"I don't believe your little sister, Steph," Darcy said. "She's really something."

"She sure is. The question is, what?" Stephanie stepped onto the down escalator and turned to face her friends.

"You really were patient with her about the barrette, though. I was impressed." Allie giggled again. "But that bra! Wouldn't you have just died if there'd been any boys you knew around to see that?"

"Speaking of boys," Darcy said. "Don't look now, Steph, but there's one coming our way."

Of course, Stephanie couldn't help looking. She turned around just in time to see Brandon Fallow riding toward them on the up escalator. Brandon was in the ninth grade and the star of the soccer team. He was tall, with dark hair and big dark eyes.

"Hi, Stephanie," Brandon said as the escalator carried him farther away. "Hi, Allie and Darce."

"Oh. Hi, Brandon." Stephanie tried to sound nonchalant as she swung back around. Once again facing her friends, she said, "Look at me. What do you see?"

"A phony smile," Allie said.

"It's not phony; it's casual," Stephanie corrected her. "Okay. What else do you see?"

"Nothing," Darcy said.

"Exactly. The *new* Stephanie, upon seeing a gorgeous specimen of the opposite sex, will no longer blush *or* giggle."

"You really *are* serious about this new Stephanie stuff, aren't you?" Darcy said.

"Absolutely," Stephanie said, stepping off the escalator. "Seventh grade, here I come!"

*   *   *

At home after the shopping spree, Stephanie lugged her bags up to the room on the second floor that she shared with her younger sister.

So far the new Stephanie project was going well, but the real challenges would come at home, where she lived with her extended family—her dad, Danny Tanner, D.J. and Michelle, her Uncle Jesse, his wife Becky, and their twin three-year-olds, Nicky and Alex. Plus her dad's friend Joey Gladstone and Comet, a golden retriever. The dog she wasn't worried about. But the humans were used to the old Stephanie— the disorganized, happy-go-lucky Stephanie. She hoped they took the new one as seriously as she did.

While Stephanie removed her new clothes from a shopping bag, Michelle entered the room and began poking around in another bag.

"So can I wear your new barrette to school tomorrow?" Michelle asked, unwrapping the tissue paper from the silver barrette.

Patience, Stephanie reminded herself. "Sorry, Michelle, but tomorrow is the first day of school, and I plan on wearing it."

"But you promised," Michelle insisted.

"You'll have plenty of chances to wear it," Stephanie told her. "Just give me some time to break it in, okay?"

"Promise?"

"Promise."

Michelle handed over the barrette. Pleased with the way she'd handled her little sister, Stephanie cut the price tags off her new clothes. Then she tacked a newly made to-do list on the bulletin board above her desk.

"What's that?" Michelle asked.

"It's called a to-do list," Stephanie explained. "Everything I need to do, I put on this list so I won't forget. 'Tuesday: Walk Comet, Wednesday: Do the dishes, Thursday: Take out the garbage.'"

"Ick!" Michelle's mouth puckered, as if she'd sucked a lemon. "Who wants to be reminded of that stuff?"

"I do. It's all part of the new me."

"The *new* you?" Michelle looked around the room, confused. "Where's the old you?"

"The old one's history."

"Like in a book?"

"No, not like in a book. The new me's different, that's all," Stephanie said patiently. "Better."

"The new you's not smiling," Michelle observed.

"That's because I have important things on my

10

mind." Stephanie ran her eyes over the list again. *Put out clothes* was written on every day except Friday and Saturday. "Right," she said. "I think I'll wear the new skirt and sweater tomorrow." She put away everything else and carefully draped the sweater and skirt over a chair for the morning—something the old Stephanie would never have done in advance.

When Stephanie looked up, Michelle was taping a crayon drawing of a smiling sun right on top of the to-do list.

Stephanie took a big breath. Why did Michelle always have to touch her things? *Stay calm, Steph,* she told herself. Then she smiled at her sister. "Michelle, what are you doing?" she asked sweetly. "You put that right on top of my list."

"I know," Michelle said. "It's to remind you of one more thing."

"What?"

"To have a nice day," Michelle said proudly.

CHAPTER
2

♦ ◀ ◼ ♦

When her alarm went off the following morning, Stephanie jumped right out of bed. *No more snooze button mornings for me,* she thought. She stretched her arms up to the ceiling. Then she went to the window and flipped up the blinds to see what the first day of seventh grade was going to be like.

It was pouring rain outside. *Oh, well, the new Stephanie can handle it,* she told herself.

Moving to her desk, she found her sister's smiling sun taped on top of her to-do list again. Stephanie had taken it down last night after Michelle fell asleep. *They'd have to have a little chat,* she thought, glancing over at her sister's empty bed. Michelle obviously didn't understand the importance of the list. Yet.

Removing the artwork, Stephanie scanned the items on her list under Monday.

One. Don't forget your bus pass.

Two. Don't forget your lunch.

Three. Don't forget the combination lock for your locker.

"That's something the old Stephanie would definitely have forgotten," Stephanie murmured.

After checking to make sure her bus pass and combination were in her book bag, Stephanie headed off to the bathroom to take a shower. There were three bathrooms in the Tanner house, but sharing them with six other people could be tricky at times. The rule on weekdays was: three-minute showers, max, and no dawdling in front of the mirror.

By the time Stephanie got to the bathroom, Michelle was already in the shower. As she stood in the hallway, waiting, three-year-old Nicky ran by in his underpants. Then Becky rushed up, waving a pair of jeans in the air. Nicky squeaked and took off down the hall.

"Oh, Stephanie!" Becky said breathlessly. "Do

me a big favor. Catch Nicky and put on his jeans for me, while I wrestle Alex into his." She handed Stephanie the jeans.

"But . . ."

Before Stephanie could finish her sentence, Becky raced back up to the top floor. "Thanks, you're a lifesaver!" she called over her shoulder.

Stephanie looked down at the tiny jeans, shook her head, and raced off to catch her little cousin.

"Nicky? Where are you?" Stephanie called out as she went downstairs to the living room. "You forgot your pants, and I don't want to be late for school."

From behind the couch she heard a little giggle. But as she went to catch Nicky, he darted out from his hiding place and ran past her into the kitchen.

"Nicky! Stop!"

Stephanie dashed into the kitchen and immediately spotted Nicky hiding under the kitchen table.

"Let's be reasonable, Nicky." Stephanie circled the table. "You're missing your pants, and I'm going to miss my bus if you don't come out."

Nicky didn't move.

"Like right this minute," Stephanie added firmly.

14

Nicky crawled out from under the table.

"Steph-nie mad at Nicky?" he said.

"No, no." Stephanie couldn't help smiling. "I'm not mad at you. It's just that, see, I'm turning over a new leaf and . . ."

Realizing she was about to explain the *new* Stephanie to a three-year-old without any pants on, she stopped herself. "Later, Nicky," she said. "For now, just let me get you dressed."

When Stephanie finally returned to the bathroom, the shower was still occupied. Thinking that Michelle was taking advantage of the three-minute rule, Stephanie barged into the bathroom.

"Okay, Michelle," she said in a calm but firm voice. "Your three *hours* in the shower are up. It's my turn."

"Michelle's gone, Steph," D.J. said, her head peeking out from behind the shower curtain. "And I still have"—she checked the imaginary watch on her wrist—"two minutes and ten seconds left."

"Sorry, D.J.," Stephanie said, backing out of the bathroom.

Stephanie finally got into the bathroom and took a shower in record time. Fifteen insane minutes later she dashed to her dad's car in the rain—trying not to panic. D.J. and Michelle had caught their school buses, but she'd missed hers.

"Dad, really. I can take the city bus," Stephanie said as she fastened her seat belt.

"No problem, Steph." Danny smiled and pulled the car onto the street. "It's your first day of school, and it's raining cats and dogs."

"Okay, but I'll take the bus home."

This is great, Stephanie thought, rolling her eyes. *My first day in seventh grade and the whole school will see my dad dropping me off. He must think I'm starting kindergarten.*

Stephanie pulled down the sun visor and checked her hair in the mirror. It was a little damp from the rain, but the new silver barrette looked great.

"Got your lunch?" Danny asked.

"Huh?" Stephanie said, adjusting the barrette.

"Your lunch. You didn't forget to bring it, did you?"

"Nope." Stephanie held up her lunch bag. "Tuna on rye and some cookies."

"No fruit?"

"Oatmeal-*raisin* cookies."

Danny nodded. "What about your new notebooks?"

16

Stephanie patted her book bag. "Right here, Dad."

"I'm impressed." Danny thought for a second as he made a right turn. "Ah-ha! How about the combination to your locker?"

Stephanie rattled off the numbers easily. "And I have it written down, too," Stephanie said, a little annoyed with her father. "Don't you remember the new me? The one you trusted with your credit card? The one who didn't go over the limit on it, or anywhere near the limit? I'm twelve now and very responsible." She flipped up the visor. "You don't have to treat me like a little girl anymore, Dad."

"Sorry. I guess it's just an old habit." Danny smiled. "I'll try harder."

"Promise?"

"Promise."

As Danny pulled the car up to the front of the John Muir Middle School, the rain turned into a downpour.

"Uh-oh," Danny said, looking worried. "Maybe I should pick you up after school."

"Dad!"

"Oh, right. You're not a little girl, sorry," Danny said, looking slightly embarrassed. "But at least take an umbrella or you'll get drenched." He fumbled around in the backseat and handed an umbrella to Stephanie as she opened the car door.

"Thanks." Stephanie stepped over a puddle of water at the curb, grabbed the umbrella, and opened it over her head. "And thanks for the lift, too, Dad," she added.

"You *sure* you don't want me to pick you up after school. . . ? Just kidding. Bye."

Stephanie laughed as she slammed the door shut.

"Steph. Steph!" a familiar voice called out. It was Allie wearing a shiny blue slicker with the hood covering her wavy hair.

"Hi, Allie," Stephanie said as she joined her. "Ready for the seventh grade?"

Allie moaned. "I can't believe it's raining on the first day of school. I mean, I can just *hear* my hair frizzing!"

As the two girls joined the crowd heading toward the school, Stephanie noticed two Flamingoes, Jenni Morris and Diana Rink, standing near the front doors.

The Flamingoes was a club that Stephanie had almost joined last year. The girls in it thought they were "ultra-cool," but as Stephanie found out, they were really "ultra-jerks." The only thing cool about them was the way they dressed. They wore lots of pink, to go with their name. And even though Stephanie had decided not to wear that color anymore, she had to admit that the Flamingoes really did know fashion. Today Diana had on black leggings under a hot-pink mini-skirt and T-shirt, and Jenni wore baggy jeans, Doc Martens, and a pink-and-white checkered shirt.

Just as Stephanie and Allie reached the top step, Jenni smirked. Diana giggled.

Stephanie looked around, but she didn't see anything amusing.

Now Diana and Jenni were both laughing. Worse, they were pointing right at Stephanie.

"I wonder what's so funny," Stephanie muttered to Allie. "Is there mud on my skirt or something?"

"Um . . ." Allie was trying not to smile. "I think it's your umbrella, Steph."

Stephanie looked up and her eyes grew wide. She couldn't believe what she saw. The umbrella was decorated with bright yellow ducks with fat orange feet. She looked at the handle, and her

19

jaw dropped in disbelief. The handle was shaped like a duck's head. Danny had given her Michelle's dumb, babyish, silly duck umbrella! *So much for not treating me like a little girl,* she thought.

Red-faced, Stephanie quickly pulled the umbrella closed and followed Allie into the building. Behind her, she could hear Jenni and Diana still laughing.

"Don't let them get to you, Steph," Allie said. "They're not worth it."

As Stephanie looked at the umbrella, she remembered her vow to be mature and handle things differently.

"You're right," she told Allie with a big smile. "It's only an umbrella."

CHAPTER
3

◆ ◀ ◆ ◆

After Stephanie stuffed the duck umbrella into her locker, she tried to forget about it. All through her morning classes, she paid attention and didn't doodle on any of her new notebooks. And when she went to her locker before lunch, remembering the combination was no problem. She quickly grabbed the tuna fish sandwich she'd fixed the night before and headed for the cafeteria.

"Hey, Steph," Darcy called. "Over here."

Darcy was waving to her from a table filled with friendly faces—Allie, of course. Plus Sue Krammer, Lizzie Timmons, and Kara Landford.

"Hi, everybody," Stephanie said as she joined them. "Is seventh grade totally cool or what?"

"Or what." Sue groaned. "It's only lunchtime and I've already got tons of homework."

"I like it so far," Allie put in. "Guess who's in my social studies class?"

"Andrew Zebell!" everybody said, so loudly that Allie blushed. She had a major crush on Andrew, but she was too shy to do anything about it.

"I like your barrette, Stephanie," Kara said.

"Thanks, Kara." Stephanie unwrapped her sandwich. "I'm so hungry I could eat a horse."

"Yeah, well, that's what you would be eating if you bought the cafeteria food: horse meat!" Darcy said, poking her fork at a dark-brown blob of something on her plate.

"Come on, Darcy." Kara took a bite of her own blob and chewed. "It's not that bad. It's some sort of chopped meat."

"Yeah, right. Mystery meat!" Lizzie replied.

"Face it, guys," Stephanie said. "Cafeteria food is cafeteria food. It's just one of those things that never change."

"Can we *change* the subject?" Sue complained. "I'm trying to eat, if you haven't noticed." Sue's lunch consisted of carrot sticks, celery sticks, and ten skinny slices of cucumber.

"Is that all you're eating?" Allie asked.

"Uh-huh," Sue said as she chomped down on a carrot. "I decided to go vegetarian this week."

"So, is anybody taking any ECCs?" Lizzie asked.

Darcy gave her a funny look. "ECCs? Is that some kind of medicine?"

"Try extracurricular courses. You take them after school."

"Extra courses? Puh-lease," Kara said. "It's only the first day of school."

"I know, but the ECCs are filling up fast," Lizzie said. "There's chess, and photography, and computer programming, and . . ."

Kara shook her head. "I'm busy after school."

Lizzie looked at Stephanie. "What about you, Steph?"

"I don't know," Stephanie said. "Last year I found out that I hated to sew. But I really want to try *some*thing."

"Why don't you try out for *The Scribe?*" Sue suggested. That's my choice. There's a meeting after school today."

"The school newspaper?" Allie nodded. "That

would be a good thing for you, Steph. You're interested in writing."

"Yeah," Stephanie agreed. Allie was right— she was interested in writing. And working on *The Scribe* would be a serious, responsible thing to do—perfect for the new Stephanie. "What made you think of it, Sue?"

"Billy Klepper's on it."

"You want to work on the paper because of a boy?" Stephanie asked.

Sue shrugged. "Tell me *you* don't have any boys on your mind, Steph."

"Me? Never," Stephanie quipped.

Darcy grinned. "Why does the name Brandon Fallow pop into my head?"

"Brandon Fallow?" Kara said. "Oooh, really, Stephanie?"

"Darcy!" Stephanie tried hard not to blush. "Brandon Fallow is not on my mind. And besides, I have a whole new attitude toward boys."

"Oh, really?" Sue raised her eyebrows.

"All I know is I'm not going to fall over my feet anymore when they're around," Stephanie announced. "It's seventh grade. Time to grow up. Be more cool."

Stephanie had barely finished the sentence

when none other than Brandon Fallow walked by. All the girls stared at him, including Stephanie.

"But I'll tell you one thing," Stephanie added with a big grin on her face. "Brandon Fallow sure is cute!"

Stephanie Tanner, ace reporter. It has a nice ring to it, Stephanie thought as she entered the school newspaper office. About fifteen students were already there, sitting around on the desks and chairs used by the newspaper staff to write and publish *The Scribe*. Although they were mostly ninth graders, Stephanie did recognize a few seventh graders, including Sue. Sue was seated in the first row, smiling at Billy Klepper, who was standing a few feet away from her.

"Aren't you in the wrong office, Steph? The cooking club is meeting down the hall." It was the unfriendly voice of Tiffany Schroeder, another Flamingo.

"No, Tiff," Stephanie answered calmly. "I happen to be in the *right* place. And by next week I expect to be sitting behind one of these desks as one of *The Scribe*'s new reporters."

Tiffany smirked. "Dream on," she said. With

a toss of her long, permed hair, she plopped down in a nearby chair.

The adviser of *The Scribe*, Mrs. Blith, introduced the current staff and welcomed the "try-outs." She explained that the paper was looking for three new permanent writers, and that anyone interested should turn in an article that reflected his or her best work by next Monday.

Stephanie decided she was definitely interested. All she had to do now was come up with a great idea for a story.

Later that evening, as the Tanners were polishing off dessert—a deep-dish apple pie that Danny had picked up at the bakery—Stephanie decided to see if they could help her think of any ideas. "Excuse me, everyone," she said. "I've got something I want to tell you."

"Order in the court," Joey said, tapping his fork on his dessert plate.

The twins beat their spoons on the table.

Stephanie raised her voice. "This is important."

"Nicky, Alex." Becky put a finger to her lips. "Shhh!"

"Shhh," the twins said back.

26

Over the shushing noises, Danny said, "Go ahead, Stephanie. Tell us."

Stephanie sat up straight in her chair. "I just wanted to tell everybody that you're looking at a soon-to-be reporter for *The Scribe.*"

"*The Scribe?* Wow, Steph!" Becky said. "That's great."

"What's a 'Scribe'?" Michelle asked.

"It's the middle school newspaper," Danny explained.

"It fits perfectly into my new plans for being a more responsible person," Stephanie went on. "Plus, I love to write. Of course, I'm not on the newspaper staff yet. First I have to write an article, and it needs to be something that will really knock everyone's socks off."

Michelle looked down at her socks. "Why do you want to do that? These are my favorite socks."

"It's a figure of speech, honey," Danny said. "It means 'great.' "

"I've got it!" Jesse jumped out of his seat. "Why not write a story about the twins? You could interview them and—"

"Maybe you haven't noticed, but the twins can barely talk," D.J. reminded Jesse.

"Oh. Right." Jesse thought for a second, then he perked up. "So? She can interview the parents!"

"Sit down, Jesse," Danny said.

"Wait a minute. Wait a minute." Joey smiled. "I've got the perfect idea. N. A. G."

"Nag?" Danny looked confused.

"That's right, N. A. G.," Joey repeated. "The National Association for Gravity."

D.J. burst out laughing. "What does it do? Send up balloons?"

"You can laugh now, but *gravity* is going to be the next great environmental issue of the day," Joey insisted. "There's already a shortage."

"You mean, pretty soon everyone will have to fall up instead of down?" Becky joked.

When the laughter died down, Michelle voiced her suggestion.

"I think she should write a story about a flower who gets picked from a garden and has to live the rest of her life in a flowerpot."

"Hmm. Cruelty to plants . . . interesting," Danny said. He bit his lip to keep from smiling.

But Stephanie wasn't amused at all. Her family was treating the whole thing like a joke.

"Well, guys," she said as she got up from the table. "I think I'll go to my room, do my homework, lay out my clothes for tomorrow, think about your wonderful ideas, and then go to sleep. See ya."

"Think *gravity*, Steph. *Gravity!*" Joey said.

"Gavity!" the twins echoed.

Everyone laughed again as Stephanie headed for her room.

Upstairs, Stephanie quickly polished off her math and English homework, then lay back on her bed and tried to come up with her own idea for *The Scribe*. She wanted to do something serious and hard-hitting. Some sort of investigative article.

Stephanie closed her eyes and tried to concentrate. She could hear Alex crying, Michelle singing a song with Danny, and D.J. talking on the phone. Then Comet barked.

Stephanie turned over and pulled the pillow on top of her head to shut out the noise. *A hard-hitting story. An exposé*, she said to herself. *But what? What could she expose at the boring old John Muir Middle School?*

Suddenly the pillow was yanked from her

head. Stephanie opened one eye and saw Michelle staring down at her.

"I want my umbrella," Michelle demanded.

"Huh?"

"My duck umbrella. Dad said he gave it to you."

"Oh, that." Stephanie suddenly remembered that she'd hidden the umbrella in her locker and forgotten about it. "Sorry, Michelle. I left it at school."

"You left *my* umbrella at school, and you wouldn't even let me borrow your barrette?" Michelle dropped the pillow back over Stephanie's head and walked out of the room in a huff.

Stephanie closed her eyes again. *Hard-hitting,* she thought. *A serious piece of journalism.*

"Steph-nie. Steph-nie," a little voice said. "It hurts. It hurts." Stephanie opened her eyes. Alex was staring at her, his lower lip stuck out. Pulling up his T-shirt, he pointed to his belly button.

"There you are, Alex," Becky said, entering the room carrying a spoon and bottle of medicine. "I want you to drink this. It's yum-yum." Becky explained to Stephanie that Alex had a stomachache.

"It's yuck. *Yuck!*" Alex insisted, tears streaming down his face.

"No, it's not, Alex. Really," Stephanie said. "Here, I'll show you. I'll take some myself." *Anything to get some peace and quiet,* she thought. She took the bottle from Becky, dabbed a tiny drop of medicine onto her little finger, and licked it off. It tasted like cherry-flavored chalk.

"Mmmm. Delicious!" she said, hoping she wouldn't gag. "Now it's Alex's turn. Open wide."

Becky poured out a spoonful of medicine and placed it in Alex's mouth.

"Mmmm. Dishis!" Alex mimicked Stephanie.

"Okay, Alex. Time to go to bed," Becky said. "Thanks, Steph. And by the way, I think you'd make a great reporter for *The Scribe.*"

"Thanks, Becky. I needed that."

Stephanie fell back on her bed and closed her eyes one more time.

I need a hard-hitting story. I need a serious subject, she told herself again. *And I need to get this terrible taste out of my mouth!*

After a trip to the bathroom to brush her teeth, she tried to think about the story again, but her mind was blank. Frustrated, she decided to call

31

it quits for the night. After all, you couldn't rush these things. She knew she'd eventually think of something.

Sliding off the bed, Stephanie checked out her to-do list. She was putting out a new green mini-skirt and a white cotton sweater for the next day, when suddenly there was a chorus of crying—both twins this time. Running upstairs to the third floor, she found Becky bending over Nicky's bed.

"Poor Nicky can't sleep, can he?" Becky said as she rearranged his blanket. Then she turned to Stephanie and whispered, "Alex's crying woke him up and now he's cranky."

Nicky whimpered. Alex wailed. *Nicky* wailed.

It's a good thing I already did my homework, Stephanie thought. Then she made a quick decision. "Hey, I have an idea," she said. "Why don't you let Nicky sleep in my bed? That way, if Alex cries in the night, maybe Nicky won't hear him."

"That's very generous, Steph," Becky said. "But where will you sleep?"

"I don't know. I guess the couch in the living room."

"You really don't mind?" When Stephanie

shook her head, Becky breathed a sigh of relief. "What would I do without you, Steph? Thanks."

It had seemed like a good idea at the time. After all, Stephanie wanted to be grown-up and mature, and that meant helping out Becky. Besides, there was no way Stephanie could sleep with both twins crying anyway. Right?

But could she sleep on the couch? she wondered. First her arm slipped through the cracks between the pillows, then her knee. If she kept twisting and turning, she'd be a pretzel by morning.

As she was finally drifting off, a loud sound bolted her up into a sitting position.

It was the front door. Joey had come home from his job as a stand-up comedian in a comedy club.

"Hi, Steph." Joey took off his jacket and tossed it onto a nearby chair. "What are you doing on the couch?"

"Trying to sleep." Stephanie rubbed her eyes. "What time is it?"

"About one o'clock."

"Terrific," Stephanie moaned, falling back onto the couch.

"Steph, wake up," Joey said, sitting next to her on the edge of the couch. "I got it! I really got it this time!"

"Good."

"No, listen. It's the perfect idea for your newspaper story."

Stephanie sat up and tried to clear her sleepy head.

"Ready for this?" Joey asked.

"Do I have any choice?"

"Okay. Okay. Two words—Alien ships." He grinned at her expectantly.

Stephanie blinked. "Alien ships?"

"Alien ships. A guy at the club told me he read about a landing in New Mexico. Said there were pictures and all. So what do you think? Wouldn't that make one heck of a story for your school paper?"

"Yeah." Stephanie closed her eyes. "I can see it, Joey. Thanks a lot."

"Anytime, Steph," Joey said as he stood up. "Good night."

"Good night," Stephanie whispered, then plopped back down onto the couch. *Alien ships. Orphaned flowers. Gravity! When will someone around here take me seriously?*

Stephanie rearranged the pillows and tossed and turned some more. She never did get comfortable, but she was so tired she managed to fall into a deep, lumpy sleep.

In what seemed like only a few minutes, a moist tongue on her cheek and warm dog breath in her face woke her up again.

"Gross! Comet, stop it. I get the message."

And Stephanie knew very well what the message was: The dog needed walking. It was five A.M. Stephanie grabbed Joey's jacket and threw it over her pajamas, then clipped the leash onto Comet's collar.

"Let's go," she told him. "And make it fast. I don't want to get too wide awake."

By the time Stephanie got back to the couch, she didn't even bother to rearrange the pillows. She fell onto them and was asleep in an instant.

About an hour later her sleep was interrupted again. This time it was the twins—well, wide-awake, and ready to play climb the mountain—using Stephanie as the mountain!

The *new* Stephanie refused to be defeated. After persuading the twins to climb on the couch pillows instead of on her exhausted body, she staggered upstairs with the thought of taking an early shower. Why not get a head start? But her bed looked so inviting, and she was still so groggy, that she couldn't resist lying down. *Just for a minute,* she promised herself as her head hit the pillow. *I'll only stay here for one minute.*

CHAPTER
4

♦ ◄ ◆ ♦

It was a very long minute. So long that when Stephanie finally woke up, it was panic city. First she couldn't find her barrette. Then she spilled orange juice. Then she almost forgot her book bag and had to make a mad dash for the late school bus, which she almost missed.

"All my careful planning was totally wasted," Stephanie told Allie as they headed for the cafeteria at lunchtime. "I hadn't even brushed my hair. I looked completely ridiculous!" She sighed. "And I was still so sleepy that I almost nodded off in math and Mr. Ryan made noises like an alarm clock at me in front of the whole class! My stomach's been doing triple flips all morning because I missed breakfast. And I forgot my lunch, so if you don't loan me a couple of bucks, I'll shrivel up and die."

"I'd never let you shrivel," Allie said as the two friends entered the cafeteria and went right onto the serving line. "Get whatever you want."

Stephanie slid her tray along the serving table, taking one of everything: a carton of milk, a small salad, and a roll.

"What's that?" she asked the lunch attendant when she reached the main course.

"Meat loaf," the attendant said.

Stephanie peered at the gray-brown slabs of meat in the warmer. "You're kidding, right?"

The attendant frowned. "Do I look like I'm kidding?" She scooped up a piece of meat from the warmer. "Do you want it or not? Make up your mind, you're holding up the line."

"Go ahead, Steph, take it," Allie said. "If you don't like it, you can always throw it away."

The attendant flashed Allie a dirty look.

"Okay. I'll take it," Stephanie said. "I need all the energy I can get."

With their trays full of food, Stephanie and Allie joined Darcy at a nearby table. Across from them were Lizzie and Sue.

"I bet I know what you were dreaming about when you nodded off in math class this morning," Lizzie said as soon as Stephanie sat down.

Darcy looked surprised. "You fell asleep in math class?"

"Please. No instant replays," Stephanie said with a yawn. "It was bad enough that I got zilch hours of sleep last night, but getting caught dozing by Mr. Ryan on the second day of school has to take some sort of prize."

"Speaking of prizes," Sue said, chewing on a celery stick, "one of the eighth graders decided not to quit *The Scribe* after all. So Mrs. Blith is only going to pick *two* seventh graders for the staff, not three."

Only two! Stephanie felt panicky for a second, but she managed to overcome it. "Well, then," she said, trying to sound calm and self-assured. "I'll have to make sure *my* story is a real blockbuster."

"Do you have any ideas yet?" Darcy asked.

"Not yet," Stephanie had to admit. "And my family's no help at all. I don't even think the *Enquirer* would print their suggestions." She forced a smile. "But I'll think of something. It just takes time."

Stephanie poked around her plate with her fork and finally decided to try the meat loaf. Just as she stuck the fork into it, Darcy yelled out, "Don't eat that!"

Stephanie almost dropped her fork. "Why not?"

"Rumor has it that the meat has been nuked," Darcy said seriously.

"Nuked?"

"You know. Microwaved," Darcy explained.

"So what?" Stephanie said. "I 'nuke' stuff all the time at home."

"Not like they do it here," Lizzie told her. "Why do you think that stuff has a greenish glow to it?"

"You're kidding."

"Let's put it this way," Darcy warned. "Eat at your own risk."

Stephanie wasn't sure if Lizzie and Darcy were serious or just pulling her leg. She took one bite of the meat loaf and found out. "Oh, gross!" She swallowed the disgusting meat and took a big gulp of milk. "How can they serve this stuff and call it food? It tastes like . . . like . . ."

"Horse meat?" Lizzie said.

Sue held up a carrot stick. "Stick with these," she advised Stephanie. "You'll live longer."

Stephanie threw down her fork and stared at her plate. Was it her imagination, or was the meat really glowing? Could there possibly be something dangerous in it? "Hey!" she cried suddenly. "That's it!"

"What? Where?" Allie said, looking around.

"I've got it!" Stephanie said excitedly.

"Got what?" Darcy asked. "Food poisoning?"

Stephanie shook her head. "No, I mean I've got an idea for a story."

"Oh, great!" Allie said. "What is it?"

Stephanie pointed dramatically to the meat loaf. "This!"

"That?" Allie looked confused.

"Yes! An exposé on cafeteria food," Stephanie explained. "Is it harmful . . . ?"

"Is it *food* would be a better question," Darcy joked.

41

"No, I really mean it," Stephanie said seri-ously. "Is the food in the cafeteria safe? Is some-body making a profit by serving cheap food? Cafeteria corruption. Deep stuff like that."

"Cool," Darcy said.

"Very!" Lizzie agreed.

"I love it," Allie said, taking a sip of milk. "I wish I'd thought of it." She groaned and ate a slice of cucumber.

Stephanie felt fantastic. She'd come up with a great idea for her story and couldn't wait to get started.

"So where do you begin?" Allie asked, as if she read her mind. "I mean, where will you get your facts?"

"Right there." Stephanie pointed to the doors leading into the cafeteria kitchen. "I saw this movie about bank robbers," she explained. "And the de-tective said that the way to solve the case was to follow the money. So, in this case, I guess I have to follow the food—right back into the kitchen."

Pushing back her chair, Stephanie took a deep breath, then headed toward the kitchen doors. Just as she reached them, Francis McDougal, the head lunch lady, came barreling out, almost knocking Stephanie over.

"Can I help you?" Francis McDougal was about forty-five years old and tough-looking, with broad shoulders and a loud voice. All the kids at school called her "Sergeant" McDougal.

"Um. Yes. Um." Stephanie thought fast. "I'd like to see how you make that delicious meat loaf," she said with a bright smile. "It's my family's favorite food, and I'd love to get your recipe so I can make it at home sometime."

"I'm afraid not, young lady," McDougal said, grabbing Stephanie's shoulders and spinning her around. "No one but cafeteria staff is permitted in the kitchen."

Stephanie had no choice but to go back to her table. Instead of feeling defeated, she felt more sure of herself than ever. "Did you see how fast Sergeant McDougal got rid of me?" she said as she sat down.

"Yeah, it was like she had something to hide," Allie said.

"Exactly!" Stephanie said. "I think I'm really on to something. There's more to this cafeteria food than meets the eye. And I'm going to get to the bottom of it!"

* * *

That afternoon Stephanie started a list of what she needed to do to get the scoop on the cafeteria food.

Number One: Get into the kitchen—somehow.

"Okay. Where is it?" Michelle said, marching into the bedroom.

"Not now, Michelle. Can't you see I'm busy with my story?" *Number Two:* Stephanie wrote.

"I don't care about your stupid story," Michelle said, putting her hands on her hips. "I just want my umbrella back."

For the second day in a row Stephanie had forgotten to bring the dumb duck umbrella home. "Sorry, Michelle. I'll bring it home tomorrow. I promise."

"I want it *now,* not tomorrow."

"Be reasonable, Michelle. There's no way I can get it for you now. And besides, you don't need it now because it's not raining."

"I'm going to tell Dad."

"Okay, go tell Dad," Stephanie said, figuring that would get her sister out of the room. As Michelle raced out, Stephanie went back to her list. *Number Two . . .*

"Steph, what do you think?" D.J. asked, coming into the room.

44

"Great. Just great, D.J."

"Steph! You didn't even look!"

Stephanie glanced up at her sister. There was something different about her hair, but she wasn't sure what. "It's perfect," she said, looking down at her list again. "It's you. Really."

"Well, thanks. I think." D.J. sounded miffed as she left.

Okay. Number Two, Stephanie said to herself one more time.

"Ice cream," a little voice said. "Ice cream."

"Oh, hi, Nicky," Stephanie said, not looking up from her notes.

"Me Alex," the little voice said. "I want ice cream."

Stephanie gave up and tossed her pencil down. "Sure, why not? Maybe ice cream will get my brain cells going."

Stephanie escorted Alex to the kitchen and pulled out a container of chocolate fudge-nut swirl from the freezer.

"This is for you," she said as she filled a bowl with a scoop of ice cream and put it on the kitchen table in front of Alex.

"And this is for me," she said, dishing out the last two scoops in the container for herself. As she sat down to eat her chocolate fudge-nut swirl, she heard the phone ring, then D.J. picked it up in the other room.

"Steph!" D.J. shouted a minute later. "It's Allie! And don't take too long!"

Stephanie stuffed a spoonful of ice cream into her mouth and went to the phone.

"Hello."

"Hello. Is this Nancy Drew?"

"Hi, Allie. I think Brenda Starr is a little more appropriate."

Allie giggled. "So how's the story going?"

"Not too well. I keep getting interrupted, as usual."

"So come over to my house," Allie suggested. "Have dinner with us, and then I'll help you with your story if you help me with the math homework."

"Thanks, Allie, but I think I'll stick around here and keep trying. Maybe tomorrow."

"Cool."

Stephanie hung up and started out of the living room. By now her ice cream would be soft, but not melted, just the way she liked it. As she walked into the kitchen, she stopped in her tracks. Michelle was in her chair, lifting a spoonful of soft—but not melted—chocolate fudge-nut swirl toward her mouth.

"Michelle!" Stephanie shouted. "What do you think you're doing?"

Michelle put the spoon in her mouth. "Eating ice cream?" she mumbled.

"*My* ice cream!"

"It was starting to melt," Michelle explained in a slightly guilty voice. "So I thought I should eat it before it turned to soup."

This was a real test for the *new* Stephanie. *I have two choices*, she thought. *Freak out. Or go over to Allie's house.*

"Hi, guys," Danny said, entering the kitchen and going right to the refrigerator. He grabbed an apple from the fruit drawer, then paused to rearrange the soda cans and milk cartons on the top shelf of the refrigerator. Danny was the neat freak in the Tanner household.

"Dad?" Stephanie said. "Can I go over to Allie's house for dinner tonight?"

"It's a school night, honey."

"I know. But after dinner Allie and I are going to do our math homework and then she's going to help me with my story. I'll be back by nine o'clock. I promise."

Danny rubbed the apple on his jeans and took a big bite. "You mean you're not going to try my new recipe for tuna-noodle surprise?" he asked.

"Surprise me another time, Dad. Okay?"

"Well, okay, but you don't know what you're missing."

Yes, I do, Stephanie thought, watching Michelle polish off the last of her ice cream.

CHAPTER
5

◆ ◀ ▸ ◆

Looking forward to some peace and quiet, Stephanie walked a few blocks to Allie's house and rang the doorbell.

"Hi, Steph," Allie greeted her. "Come on in."

Stephanie followed Allie into the living room, plopped down on the soft white couch, and sighed. "Am I glad to be here!"

"So why the change of mind? Did you smell my mom's roast chicken?"

"No, but I do now," Stephanie said, sniffing appreciatively. "You know, Allie, you're lucky you don't live in a house full of people."

"Sometimes I wish I did," Allie confided. "I

mean, I love my mom and dad, but I always have a great time at your house. It's so . . ."

"Crowded!" Stephanie said. "I can't get a single second to myself anymore. And every time I try to think about my story, somebody else is in my face."

Allie laughed. "Well, relax and get ready for a fabulous dinner. Roasted, not nuked."

As Stephanie sat at the dining room table with the Taylors, she couldn't help but think how different it was at their house. "You know, at home I have to set a table for nine people," she said, unfolding a mint-green linen napkin and putting it in her lap. "There's barely enough silverware to go around."

"I know what you mean," Mrs. Taylor said sympathetically. "I came from a large family, too."

"Mom has three brothers and two sisters," Allie explained.

"Then I guess you do know what it's like, Mrs. Taylor," Stephanie said. "Waiting in line to take a shower, not getting to the refrigerator in time to get the last piece of pie, and constantly being interrupted."

"Sounds just like my in-laws." Mr. Taylor

50

chuckled and passed the crisply roasted chicken to Stephanie.

As they ate, Stephanie noticed more differences between her home and the Taylors'. She was drinking out of a crystal glass instead of a Batman mug. The silverware matched. There was no dog begging for parts of her meal. Most of all, it was quiet. If she lived in a place like this, she'd probably earn the Pulitzer Prize for journalism by the time she was fourteen.

"Well, Stephanie," Mrs. Taylor interrupted her thoughts. "Allie tells me you're trying out for the school newspaper."

Stephanie nodded. "I love to write, and working on the paper would be really great. But so far, I haven't had much chance to think about my story. I want to write one about the cafeteria food—it's totally horrible."

"It was in my day, too," Mr. Taylor said with a laugh.

"But what if it's more than that? I mean, what if the cafeteria has something to hide?" Stephanie asked. "If it does, I want to expose it. That's what my story's going to be about."

"Well, it sounds exciting," Mrs. Taylor said. "Don't forget to investigate every possibility.

Don't believe everything you hear. Stick to the facts and write from the heart." She smiled and passed Stephanie a bowl of potatoes. "If you need any help, just give a yell. I was the editor of my college paper."

"Thanks, Mrs. Taylor." *What a change from home*, Stephanie thought. Mrs. Taylor was taking her seriously. She actually understood how important this was.

After dinner Stephanie helped Allie clear the table and do the dishes. It was a breeze compared to the load she would have had to deal with at home. Once the kitchen was cleaned up, they went to Allie's room to do their homework, which they finished in record-breaking time—without *one* interruption.

"Okay, math is history," Allie said. "Now for your story."

"Great!" Stephanie pulled out her notes. "So far I've got *Number One: Get into the kitchen—somehow.*"

"Right, you can't expose anything if you can't see anything," Allie agreed. "Why don't you just tell Sergeant McDougal that you're doing a sort of human-interest story on the cafeteria and you'd like to observe them at work?"

"Yeah, but if they've got something to hide, then Sergeant McDougal will tell me to forget it."

"Right," Allie said again. "Maybe you could get one of the other lunch ladies to talk to you."

"You mean like, be an 'unnamed source'?"

Allie nodded.

"It's a good idea," Stephanie agreed. "But I wouldn't know who to trust. And besides, I really think I need to see things for myself." She closed her eyes. When she opened them, they were sparkling. "I've got it!" she said. "Why didn't I think of this before?"

"Think of what?"

"Well, the cafeteria kitchen's not *always* busy, right? I mean, there are probably hours and hours when nobody's in there at all!" Stephanie said excitedly. "So, I'll just wait until it's empty, and then I'll go on an ultra-secret reconnaissance mission."

Allie cocked an eyebrow. "You want to translate that?"

Stephanie grinned. "I'll sneak in!"

"Good to have you back, Steph," Danny greeted her as she walked into the kitchen at nine o'clock. "You don't know what you missed for dinner."

53

"You don't *want* to know what you missed," D.J. added.

"Tuna Catastrophe," Joey said.

"Hey, it wasn't *that* bad." Danny paused and looked around. "Was it?"

"Yes!" everyone chorused.

"So much for the tuna." Danny frowned. "Maybe it was the sour pickles." He reached into the refrigerator and pulled out an almost-full casserole dish. "Here, Steph," he said, holding the dish out to her. "You give it a taste. Tell me what you think."

"Uh, no, thanks, Dad," Stephanie said quickly. "I've got to make some notes on my investigative story."

"Come on, just one bite," Danny pleaded.

"And then you can help me with my hair," D.J. said. "If you do, I'll let you wear my suede jacket."

"Don't let her have your jacket, D.J.," Michelle warned. "She may never give it back. She still hasn't brought home my umbrella."

Stephanie ignored Michelle. "Sorry, I can't deal with your hair tonight, D.J.," she said. "I've got to work on my story."

"Yeah, leave her alone," Joey said. "She's

doing a story on alien ships that landed in New Mexico.''

"No, she's not," Michelle said. "She's writing a story about a flower that—''

"Hold it!" Stephanie put her hands up. "I'm not doing either of those stories. I have my own ideas, and what I really need now is some peace and quiet so I can concentrate. So could you all just leave me alone?''

"I'll leave you alone when I get my umbrella back," Michelle said.

Joey shrugged. "Okay, Steph, but I still think the alien ship story is the way to go.''

"You know, that's what's wrong with this family," Stephanie said. She knew she didn't sound as calm as the new Stephanie was supposed to. But she couldn't help it, especially after the peaceful evening she'd just spent at the Taylors'. "Nobody ever takes anything seriously.''

"Well, excuse us for living," D.J. said.

Michelle frowned. "You're really a grump, Stephanie.''

"Don't you think you're being a little hard on everyone, Steph?" Danny said. "We're just trying to be helpful. That's the way we are.''

"I'm sorry, Dad. It's just that I'm serious about

this story, and you guys all think it's a joke. Plus, I need space to work and quiet to think. Is that asking too much?"

"I guess not," Danny admitted.

"Thank you." Stephanie strode to the door. Then she stopped and turned around. "You know," she added, "this might be a good time for *everyone* in this house to turn over a new leaf!"

CHAPTER
6

◆ ◀ ◢ ◆

The next day at school Stephanie couldn't wait to put her plan into action. Sitting impatiently through her morning classes, she actually caught herself doodling on a notebook cover. At lunchtime she huddled with Allie and Darcy, going over the details of her reconnaissance mission. In science class she fidgeted through a boring video on the life of the fruit fly. At last it was time for her library study period.

In the library Stephanie spent exactly five minutes staring into an encyclopedia. Then she grabbed her book bag and went up to the desk. The librarian was busy and gave her a hall pass without asking any questions. As Stephanie left the library, Allie peeked over the cover of her own research book and gave her a thumbs-up.

Looking purposeful, Stephanie strode down the hall, turned a corner, and boldly entered the cafeteria. The chairs were upended on the tables. The floor was still damp from mopping. Nobody was in sight.

Stephanie made a beeline for the kitchen doors and paused just outside, holding her breath. Not a sound. Just as she'd expected. So far, so good. All she had to do was go in, take a quick—but thorough—look around, and she'd be back in the library in a flash. With the scoop of the year, she hoped.

Slowly pushing open the doors, Stephanie entered the danger zone.

Inside at last, Stephanie thought as she scanned the dimly lit room. There were yards of stainless steel counters, huge metal pots, a restaurant-sized refrigerator, and two of the biggest microwave ovens she'd ever seen.

Advancing into the room, Stephanie wiped her finger along the counters and inside some of the pots. To her disappointment, she discovered that they'd been scrubbed clean. She peered into the microwave ovens. They didn't look that different from the one in her family's kitchen, just much bigger.

Maybe I should be looking for bugs. Or cans of food with poison labels on them, Stephanie thought. One by one she opened the metal cabinets. But all she found were rows of canned peaches, cartons of powdered mashed potatoes, and boxes of instant tapioca pudding. She noticed the week's menu was taped to the freezer door, and checked it for tomorrow's lunch.

"Hmm, Salisbury steak. I better make sure I pack a lunch," she murmured.

Determined to find something incriminating, Stephanie circled the kitchen, opening the cabinets again, poking behind the cans, even checking the electrical cords on the microwaves to see if they were frayed. They weren't. In fact, everything seemed to be in order. *But it couldn't be,* she told herself. *If things were so shipshape, why had Sergeant McDougal hustled her out of here so fast?*

Frustrated, Stephanie stood in the middle of the clean kitchen floor and looked around. And that's when she saw it. A piece of bread, poking out from under one of the cabinets. Her heart thumping with anticipation, Stephanie reached down and picked it up.

The bread was covered with a whitish-gray mold.

"Bingo!" Stephanie said out loud. She had it. She had her evidence!

Eager to get out now that she'd accomplished her mission, Stephanie quickly wrapped the bread in a tissue and slipped it into her book bag. She was almost to the door when it swung open from the outside, missing her nose by inches. Gasping, she jumped back. Then she froze in her tracks.

Francis McDougal was standing in the doorway, staring at her with suspicious eyes. *I'm in trouble now*, Stephanie thought.

"What are you doing in here?" McDougal demanded.

"Um." This was one detail Stephanie hadn't worked out—an excuse in case she got caught. "I was just . . ."

"Just what?"

"Just . . . looking around," Stephanie said lamely.

"Aren't you the girl who was in here yesterday? Giving me some silly story about how your family liked meat loaf?"

"Meat loaf? Oh, right. Meat loaf. That was me."

"I see. And you are?"

"Stephanie Tanner."

Mrs. McDougal pulled a pad from her pocket and scribbled Stephanie's name in it.

I'm in big trouble, Stephanie thought.

"Come with me, Stephanie Tanner."

Two minutes later Stephanie was standing in Principal Thomas's office.

"I'm surprised at you, Stephanie," Mr. Thomas said from behind his immaculate desk. Stephanie was so nervous, her stomach was doing double flips. "Snooping around in a restricted area is serious business. There's machinery in there that could be dangerous. What do you have to say for yourself?"

"Not much," Stephanie told him, trying to keep her voice from shaking. "I—"

Suddenly the bell rang, signaling the end of the class period. *Saved by the bell*, Stephanie thought in relief. But as soon as she turned to leave, Principal Thomas spoke up.

"One moment, young lady." He pulled a pen from the desk drawer and scribbled a note.

Now I'm in really big trouble, Stephanie thought.

61

"All right, Stephanie," Mr. Thomas said, putting the note in an envelope. "I've decided to let the punishment fit the crime."

"Punishment?" Stephanie's stomach went into triple flips.

"Since you seem bent on getting into the kitchen, I'm assigning you to two days of assisting the kitchen staff, with your father's permission, of course." Mr. Thomas handed Stephanie the envelope. "You'll report to Mrs. McDougal at lunchtime tomorrow." He smiled. "Have a nice day."

Blushing with humiliation, Stephanie stepped out of the principal's office and practically collapsed against Allie and Darcy, who'd been waiting for her in the hallway.

"Boy, do you look awful!" Darcy said bluntly.

"Not as awful as I feel," Stephanie said.

"I thought I'd die when I saw McDougal marching you down the hall," Allie told her. "What happened?"

"She caught me redhanded. It was the most embarrassing moment of my life!" Stephanie moaned. "And I was just leaving, too. I'd found the bread, and I was walking to the door when all of a sudden—"

"Hold it," Darcy said. "Go back to the part about the bread."

"Yeah, what bread?" Allie asked.

Suddenly Stephanie's face lit up. "This!" she said, reaching into her book bag and pulling out the small bundle. Carefully unwrapping the tissue, she held it out for her friends to inspect. "One moldy piece of bread!"

"Definitely moldy," Darcy observed, wrinkling her nose. "*Definitely* not for human consumption. I think you've got a case, Steph."

"Yeah, the only problem is this," Stephanie lamented, showing them the envelope.

"Oh-oh. Trouble city," Darcy said. "Are you suspended?"

Allie gasped.

"Worse."

Allie gasped again. "What could be worse?"

With a grim smile Stephanie handed over the letter. "Read it and weep."

"Two days?" Allie exclaimed, reading the letter over Darcy's shoulder. "You have to work *two days* in the cafeteria kitchen?"

"Not only that, but she'll be working for Sergeant McDougal," Darcy said. "You're right, Steph. This is worse than being suspended."

Stephanie nodded. "Can you believe it? After Mr. Thomas finished sentencing me, he actually told me to have a nice day!"

Darcy handed the letter back. "I'd fight it," she said. "Take it all the way to the Supreme Court if I had to. You have rights, you know."

"Yeah, but my dad would have to be on my side," Stephanie said. "And I have a feeling he'll think this is the perfect punishment." As she put the letter back in her book bag, she suddenly thought of something. "Hey, wait a sec! Maybe it is!"

"Maybe what is what?" Allie asked.

"The perfect punishment! Remember what I said the other day—that I have to follow the food?"

Darcy nodded. "Yeah, but that didn't mean becoming a lunch lady."

"Why not?" Stephanie asked. "It's the perfect cover. One piece of moldy bread isn't enough. I need more evidence, and what's the best way to find it?"

"By being a lunch lady!" Allie said excitedly.

Darcy smiled. "Great idea, Steph!"

Stephanie laughed. "Sergeant McDougal doesn't know it, but she actually did me a favor!"

*   *   *

By the time Stephanie got home, she was feeling excited about her punishment. Now she had to convince her dad that it was a good thing. She found him in the living room, alphabetizing the magazines on the coffee table.

"Dad, can I talk to you for a moment?" Stephanie said, sitting down on the edge of the couch.

"Sure, Steph, what's up?"

"You have to sign this note from school, but before I show it to you, let me explain. Remember the story I'm writing to get on the school newspaper?"

"You mean the one about the alien ships?"

"No." *Patience*, Stephanie told herself. "That was Joey's idea. My idea is to do a hard-hitting exposé on the cafeteria food at school."

"Now, that's a meaty subject, ha, ha."

"I'm serious, Dad."

"Sorry. I couldn't resist." Danny put aside a stack of magazines and sat on one of the chairs. "Go ahead, honey. You have my full attention."

"So as part of my investigation I . . . uh . . ." Stephanie paused. "Isneakedintothecafeteriakitchentolookaround," she finished in a rush.

Danny stared at her. "Was that one word or five?"

65

"Okay, okay," Stephanie said. "I sneaked into the cafeteria kitchen to look around. It's actually nine words," she added helpfully.

"Yes, I can count." Danny was beginning to look suspicious. "And?"

"And?" Stephanie said brightly.

"Come on, Steph. There's more, isn't there?"

"Just a little." Stephanie paused again. "Only three words this time: I got caught."

"You got caught."

Wordlessly Stephanie handed Danny the letter.

"Hmm." Danny looked up from reading it. "This is *serious* stuff, Stephanie."

"But, Dad, listen!" Stephanie jumped up from the couch. "It's not all bad. See, if I can work in the cafeteria kitchen, I'll be right where I want to be! It's like I'll be undercover, but nobody will know. And I might be able to find more evidence for my story."

"*More* evidence?"

"That's the best part. While I was looking around before I got caught, I found this!" Reaching into her book bag, Stephanie pulled out the moldy bread, unwrapped it, and handed it to her father.

As Danny was examining the bread, Joey came into the living room. "Hi, Steph. Danny. What's that?"

"A piece of moldy bread. Stephanie found it in the school kitchen," Danny explained.

"No kidding? Let me see it." Joey took the bread and examined it. "Whoa! You could make a lot of penicillin with this."

"Hi, gang!" D.J. came into the room, followed by Michelle. "What's *that?*"

"A piece of moldy bread," Joey said.

"Yuck." D.J. wrinkled her nose.

"Let me see. Let me see," Michelle insisted.

Before Stephanie could stop him, Joey handed the bread to Michelle. "It just looks like white fuzz to me," she said.

"That's all it is, Michelle," Stephanie said. "Now let me have it."

Michelle held the bread behind her back. "If I give it to you, will you give me my duck umbrella?" she asked teasingly.

The duck umbrella. Stephanie had forgotten all about it. Again. "You'll get your umbrella tomorrow. I absolutely promise. Now let me have the bread."

"Oh, all right." But before Michelle could turn

over the bread, Comet trotted up behind her and snatched it from her hands.

"Comet, no, that's my evidence!" Stephanie shouted, kneeling down and grabbing the dog's collar. "No, Comet, no!"

But it was too late. Comet had swallowed the moldy slice of bread in one gulp. Now he was licking his chops and sniffing around for more.

"That's going to be one healthy dog," Joey said with a chuckle. "Hey, maybe we've got the makings for a new dog food." He snapped his fingers. "I've got it! A Moldy Munchie a day keeps the dog doctor away."

Michelle laughed hysterically. D.J. joined in, and so did Danny and Joey. Even the dog looked as if he was grinning.

Stephanie stood up and folded her arms across her chest. "I don't see what's so funny," she said through gritted teeth.

"I'm sorry, honey." Danny wiped the tears from his eyes. "It's just that Comet . . . the bread . . . the Moldy Munchie . . . the whole situation is just . . ." Danny broke down and started laughing again.

"This is not funny!" Stephanie shouted angrily. "This is absolutely, totally *un*funny!"

Everybody stared at her, smiles still on their faces.

"What do you mean, Steph?" D.J. said. "It was hilarious."

"Oh, sure!" Stephanie snapped. "Why should I expect any of you to understand? Just go ahead and laugh. Everybody around here thinks I'm a joke anyway!"

Stephanie stormed out of the living room and headed up the stairs. *Calm down! Calm down!* she kept telling herself.

Instead of going to her room, Stephanie went to her dad's study. She sat down at his desk and stared at a photograph of the entire Tanner extended family. *I can't believe it,* she thought. *I've been trying so hard to change and become more mature. And what does my family do? Treat me like I'm one of Joey's new comedy routines.*

She took a deep breath, then picked up the phone on the desk. *I've got to get out of here,* she thought, *or I'll so bonkers.* Quickly she punched in Allie's number.

"Hello, Allie? It's me, Steph. Would you mind if I camped out at your house for a few days? Maybe even a few years!"

"Sounds serious."

"It is. You won't believe what just happened. I could kill Michelle!"

"What did she do now?"

"Allie, the evidence is gone. Eaten!"

"Michelle ate the moldy bread?" Allie said in disbelief.

"No. Comet ate it. In one gulp. So much for man's best friend!"

"Steph, pull yourself together. You're not making any sense."

"It's impossible to make any sense in this place, Allie."

"That bad, huh?"

"Definitely worse!"

"Gosh, maybe you *should* come over," Allie said. "I'll clear it with my mom."

"Thanks, Allie. You're a real friend."

Allie called back almost immediately. It was okay with her mom if it was okay with Stephanie's dad. One down, one to go, Stephanie thought.

Still furious, she went up to her room, hastily stuffing clothes into her duffel bag, when Danny stuck his head around the door.

"Listen, sweetheart," he said apologetically. "I'm really sorry that we laughed. We weren't laughing

70

at *you*, though. We were laughing at the situation. But we were wrong. I guess we just didn't stop to think how important the story is to you."

"Well, I'm sorry, too," Stephanie said, taking her to-do list off the wall. "I'm sorry that I thought anybody here would even care about my story."

"Come on. That's not fair. We care. We really do, but sometimes we forget to show it."

Stephanie rolled up her list and put a rubber band around it. *Boy, if that's not the understatement of the year*, she thought.

"But about your story," Danny said. Stepping into the room, he took Mr. Thomas's letter out of his shirt pocket and handed it to Stephanie. "May you find a whole *loaf* of moldy bread tomorrow."

"Thanks." Stephanie stuffed the letter in her duffel bag.

"Uh, Steph?"

"What?"

"I can't help noticing that you're packing."

"You're right." Stephanie zipped the bag and turned around to face her father. Taking a deep breath, she said, "I want to stay at Allie's house until I get my story done."

Danny put his hands in his pockets. "Gee, honey, that's kind of drastic, isn't it?"

"I don't think so. I mean, it's not like I'm running away or anything, and Mrs. Taylor says it's okay with her if it's okay with you," Stephanie said. "Like I've been telling you, this story is super important to me. And the only way I'll ever get it done is by going to Allie's."

"You're sure it's not Mrs. Taylor's cooking?" Danny asked kiddingly.

Stephanie almost smiled. "No, Dad."

Hands in his pockets, Danny walked around the room for a moment, thinking. Stephanie waited. She'd never go without permission, but she wouldn't stay without a fight.

Finally Danny stopped pacing. "Okay, honey. I think it might be good for you. You can stay at Allie's on two conditions."

"What?"

"One: Mind your manners. Two . . ." Danny smiled and gave her a kiss on the cheek. "Come back to us soon."

CHAPTER
7

♦ ◄ ◆ ♦

"Okay. Give me *all* the gory details," Allie said when she opened her door to Stephanie fifteen minutes later.

Stephanie trudged into the living room, plopped her duffel bag down on the floor and herself onto the couch. "I'm showing the bread to Dad, right? He's looking at it while I tell him about going undercover tomorrow. Joey comes in. Dad gives the bread to Joey. D.J. and Michelle come in. Joey gives the bread to Michelle, who won't give it back to me. Comet comes in and eats it right out of her hands!" Stephanie stood up, still furious. "And everybody laughs!"

"No!"

"Yes." Stephanie sighed. "I'm just one big joke to them."

"Then what happened?"

"It wasn't pretty, that's for sure. I totally lost my cool and yelled at everyone. Then I told Dad I wanted to stay with you until the story was done, and here I am."

"Wow! That took guts, Steph."

Stephanie took a deep breath. "Tomorrow, when I work in the cafeteria, I'll get all the evidence I need. Then we'll see who's laughing!"

"Good attitude," Allie said. "Come on. I'll show you where you're staying."

"You mean I'm not staying in your room?" Stephanie looked surprised.

"Mom thought you should have some privacy. She said something about it helping the creative juices flow."

"Your mom is right," Stephanie said as she followed Allie up a flight of stairs. "And I didn't even have to explain it to her. Amazing!"

Allie opened a door at the far end of the hallway. "We had the attic redone when my uncle Vinny came to stay last summer," she said, leading the way up a steep flight of stairs. "Now it's all yours."

"*All* mine? You don't know how good that sounds."

"*Voilà!*" Allie announced, reaching the top step.

The room was fairly small, with slanted ceilings, a couple of windows, a bed, a dresser, a desk and chair, and a faded Indian rug on the floor.

"Wow!" Stephanie dropped her bag and walked into the middle of the room. "My own room!"

"You like it?" Allie asked. "It's not too cramped?"

"Are you kidding? You don't know cramped until you've shared a room with Michelle the bread-snatcher." Stephanie sat on the bed and bounced up and down a few times.

"Sorry, it's a little lumpy."

"Will you stop apologizing? It's perfect. Totally perfect!" Stephanie stretched out, tucked her hands behind her head, and stared up at the slanted ceiling. "Listen."

"What?"

"Shhh. Just listen."

Allie listened. "I don't hear anything."

"Neither do I." Stephanie smiled. "Isn't it great?"

"You'll get used to it."

Still smiling, Stephanie got up and tossed her duffel bag on the bed. She unzipped it, pulled out her to-do list, and tacked it on a bulletin board over the desk.

"What's that?" Allie asked, coming over to look at it.

"My to-do list. It's supposed to help me get things done. You know, keep me organized and stuff. But it hasn't been much help so far," Stephanie admitted.

"So do you have a plan for tomorrow?" Allie asked.

"Yeah. Turn the cafeteria kitchen upside down until I find something."

Later that night Stephanie changed into her nightshirt, smiling with satisfaction. She'd finally come up with a title for her story: "Cafeteria Food May Be Hazardous to Your Health." Of course, she didn't have her evidence, thanks to Michelle and Comet. But she was positive she'd find something more tomorrow. In the meantime, she'd made an outline. All she'd have to do was fill in the blanks—Who? What? Where? When? And why?

After crossing to the bed, she slipped under

the covers and turned out the bedside lamp. *It is so unbelievably quiet up here*, she thought, bunching up her pillow. *Total luxury!*

Stephanie smoothed out her pillow and flipped it over. Peace and quiet. Privacy. Just what she needed. At home she'd have been interrupted a zillion times and would never have finished the outline. Coming to Allie's was one of the best ideas she'd ever had.

Flipping her pillow back to the other side, she closed her eyes. Almost immediately she opened them again. Was that a noise? Stephanie listened for a moment, then shook her head. Nope. She must have imagined it. *Sleep, Steph*, she told herself. *You've got a big day tomorrow.*

Stephanie closed her eyes again. A few very quiet minutes went by. Then a few more. She turned on her stomach and pulled the pillow over her head, trying to drown out . . . what? Silence was all she could hear.

She reached over and flipped the light back on. Maybe she'd read for a while. After all, she never got the chance to keep the light on late when she was at home, sharing a room with Michelle.

Stephanie picked up her paperback book and

read a few lines, but she couldn't concentrate. It was too quiet!

She reached over and flipped off the light again. Maybe she'd be able to sleep now.

But hours later Stephanie was still tossing and turning.

"Steph, Steph!" Allie was shaking her gently. "Time to get up. It's seven-thirty."

"It can't be," Stephanie mumbled groggily. "The last time I looked at the clock, it was only three."

"Three? You were awake at three in the morning?"

Stephanie sat up and blinked. "Yeah," she said with a big yawn. "I guess I was too excited about tomorrow to go to sleep."

"Well, tomorrow's here," Allie said. "Come on, lunch lady. It's time to find some more evidence!"

At precisely eleven-fifteen that morning, Stephanie pushed open the double doors into the cafeteria kitchen. Her nearly sleepless night was forgotten. Her heart was pumping. She was ready to get her scoop!

The first thing Stephanie noticed was that the kitchen was really jumping. Mrs. McDougal and five of her soldiers were scurrying around, stirring mounds of mashed potato flakes into huge pots of water, moving hot food out of the huge microwaves, and shoving frozen foods in.

The second thing Stephanie noticed was that it was about a hundred degrees in the place and the air was thick with the smell of Salisbury steaks. She was starving, and she was hot. Her stomach started churning and her face broke out in a sweat.

Get a grip, Steph, she told herself. *You've got work to do. Evidence to uncover. Dirt to find!*

Suddenly Mrs. McDougal noticed her. "Listen up, everyone!" she barked. "We've got an extra hand today." The five other workers paused for a split second and smiled at Stephanie. "Here, Tanner, put this on," McDougal said, holding out a white apron that was as big as a circus tent. When Stephanie finally got it wrapped around her—twice—it almost reached the toes of her sneakers.

Next Mrs. McDougal had Stephanie put on a pair of clear plastic gloves. They looked like Baggies with fingers.

"Now this." McDougal smiled grimly and held out a hair net.

Stephanie took a step backward. "Do I have to wear that? It'll mess up my hair."

"This isn't a beauty contest, Miss Tanner. Wear it. It's Department of Health regulations."

"Terrific," Stephanie muttered under her breath as she tried to get the hair net to stay on her head. McDougal helped her, pushing about ten bobby pins in it to keep it in place.

"Okay, Tanner, you're ready for the world of work. Start over there," McDougal ordered, pointing to a stainless steel counter filled with oversize cans of peaches and little white cups. "Peaches in the cups. Easy, right? Three per cup. No more, no less. Got it?"

"Got it," Stephanie said. Trying not to trip on the apron, Stephanie scanned the room for clues on her way to the peaches. As she passed by one of the large microwave ovens, she caught her reflection in it and froze. *Oh, my gosh! I look like . . . like one of Joey's aliens!* She wanted to crawl under a rock. Unfortunately, there weren't any.

"Move it, Tanner!" McDougal barked. "You've got peaches to dish out. Cups to fill."

Evidence to find, Stephanie thought. Hiking up

the skirt of the apron, she hurried to the counter and got to work. After filling what seemed like a zillion paper cups with canned peaches, McDougal had her fill others with mashed potatoes. Stephanie worked as fast as she could, but whenever McDougal turned her back, she looked around for clues.

"Tanner!"

Stephanie jumped and slammed the refrigerator door.

"What are you looking for?"

"Nothing, Mrs. McDougal." The only scoop she'd gotten so far was the one she'd used to dish out the potatoes.

"Here." McDougal handed Stephanie two pot holders and then stuck a tray filled with hot Salisbury steaks into Stephanie's Baggie-covered hands. "Put these onto the serving line and take over for Rosie."

Stephanie's mouth dropped open. "Out there? With all the kids?"

"They're the ones eating the food. Now go. Go! Go! Go!" McDougal gave Stephanie a push toward the kitchen door.

Suddenly Stephanie found herself standing in front of the entire student body at John Muir

Middle School. *Please*, she thought. *Please don't let anybody recognize me.*

"Hey guys, look!" Jenni Morris said as she slid her tray up to Stephanie. "It's Stephanie Tanner, modeling the latest in kitchenwear!"

Diana Rink smirked. "Love your hair, Steph!" she said, loud enough for the entire world to hear.

Stephanie felt her face get hot and knew she looked like a tomato with a fishnet stuck on it. But all she could do was dish out Salisbury steaks and hope that Brandon Fallow had brought his own lunch from home.

"Steph? What have they done to you?" Allie said as she moved down the line.

"Please, Allie, you're my best friend. Tell me I don't look as ridiculous as I think I do!"

Allie opened her mouth, but no words came out.

"Never mind," Stephanie said. "I won't ask you to lie for me."

"What are you doing out here?" Allie asked. "You're supposed to be looking for clues in the kitchen."

"Tell me about it," Stephanie said. "I *was* trying to find some evidence. But Sergeant McDougal thought I was goofing off, so she sent me out here—looking like this!"

"Never mind how you look." Allie leaned close and dropped her voice to a whisper. "Did you find anything yet?"

"So far, zip," Stephanie said. "Where's Darcy?"

"She brought her lunch. So did I," Allie said. "I only got in line when I saw you. I'm going to go eat now. Talk to you later, and good luck!"

As Allie left the line, Sue Krammer pulled her tray up to Stephanie. "Now that's an interesting fashion statement."

Stephanie decided to ignore that comment. "What are you doing here, Sue? I thought this was your vegetarian week."

"It was. Now I'm into meat and potatoes." Sue placed her tray on top of the partition between her and Stephanie. The tray was crowded with two pieces of chocolate fudge cake, three cups of peaches, and two more of mashed potatoes. "Let me have one of those brown things you're serving."

Stephanie dished up a Salisbury steak. "You sure about this?"

"I'm sure. I've got to build up my strength if I ever want to get on the soccer team."

"The soccer team?" Stephanie knew that Sue was not the athletic type.

"Yeah. I just found out Billy Klepper's a soccer freak. Maybe I'll take another one of those," she said, pointing to the warmer.

Stephanie rolled her eyes, then scooped up a second Salisbury steak from the warmer and plopped them both on Sue's plate. At that moment someone accidentally bumped into Sue from behind. As Sue lunged forward, her tray slipped from her hands and bounced over the partition.

Food flew through the air. A peach bounced off Stephanie's nose. A Salisbury steak hit her in the chest, leaving a large gravy stain on her otherwise white apron. A piece of chocolate cake landed on one shoulder, and a scoop of mashed potatoes came to rest on the other.

"What's going on here?" the familiar bark rang out in Stephanie's ear. Mrs. McDougal was standing right next to her.

"Sorry, Steph," Sue said. She frowned at the kid who'd bumped into her and left the line.

"It was an accident," Stephanie told Mrs. McDougal.

"Disaster is more like it." Sergeant McDougal

84

chuckled grimly. "Never mind. Go into the kitchen and help Rosie start the cleanup."

Glad to be back in the kitchen, Stephanie thought she would finally be able to look for clues. But after she wiped the steak gravy off her apron, Rosie kept her busy scouring the counters.

By the time lunchroom duty was over, Stephanie hadn't found a single piece of evidence. She unwrapped herself from the filthy apron, tossed the Baggie gloves into a trash can, grabbed her book bag, and fled the kitchen to go to her next class.

Halfway down the hall she realized why everyone was staring at her: She still had the hideous hair net on.

I can't believe it, she thought, changing directions and heading for her locker. *I was actually about to walk around with a fishnet on my head!*

"Steph! Slow down!" Allie called out, catching up to her friend. "How'd it go?" Allie stared at her hair. "Do you realize you're walking around with a fishnet on your head?"

"I know, I know!" Stephanie groaned. "Besides that, I'm a flop as an investigative reporter. I can't believe Sue picked today to go on a high-cholesterol, high-protein diet!"

As they walked, Stephanie kept tugging on the hair net, trying to get it loose. Instead, it just got hopelessly tangled in her long blond hair. One look at herself in the mirror attached to the inside of her locker door confirmed her worst fears.

"I look like a zombie! Allie, help!"

"Don't panic, we'll have you back to normal in no time."

"Make it faster than that, will you?"

"Just hold still." Allie started yanking bobby pins from Stephanie's tangled hair while Stephanie started gobbling the peanut butter sandwich she'd brought for lunch.

Suddenly Stephanie cried out. "Oh, no!"

"Now what?" Allie asked.

"Brandon Fallow!" Stephanie stuffed her sandwich back in the locker and spun around. "And he's headed this way!"

"I thought you weren't going to blush around boys anymore."

"I'm not blushing, I'm panicking. And this is no time to be discussing this." The hair net was only halfway off her head. Quickly Stephanie pulled Michelle's duck umbrella from her locker and popped it open, holding it so low it rested on her head and hid her face. She hoped.

86

"Let's go," she said.

Allie grabbed Stephanie by the arm and guided her down the hall toward the girls' bathroom. "This is what I call really going undercover!" She giggled.

Stephanie peeked out from under the umbrella as they scurried past Brandon. He smiled, but didn't say anything. Stephanie breathed a little easier. He probably hadn't recognized her at all.

Finally they reached the bathroom. Just as they were about to go in, the door opened and Jenni came out.

"Stephanie Tanner!" Jenni said loudly. "Haven't you noticed? It's not raining in here!"

Giggling at the stupid joke, Jenni sashayed down the hall. Stephanie snuck a glance back at her and caught sight of Brandon instead, who was standing in the middle of the hall. He was staring at Stephanie with a big grin on his face.

CHAPTER
8

♦ ◣ ◆ ♦

"Today will go down in history as the worst day in my life!" Stephanie said, collapsing onto the soft white couch in the Taylors' living room.

"Come on, it wasn't *that* bad," Darcy said, sitting cross-legged on the floor. "Remember the time you lost one of the twins and Becky and Jesse got so mad at you?"

"Right," Allie agreed, sitting next to Stephanie. "And the time you almost took your dad's long-distance calling card because you wanted to join the Flamingoes? And—"

"Okay, okay," Stephanie said. "I get the picture. I've had worse days. But not many. And I still want to die every time I think of Brandon Fallow. He actually saw me with a hair net on my head!"

Allie giggled. "No, he didn't. He saw you with a duck umbrella on your head."

Darcy laughed. "Come on. Let's watch some TV."

Trying to forget the day's miserable events, Stephanie paged through the program guide to see what was on TV.

At last! she thought as Allie turned on the television. *No more battling Michelle over what to watch—rock videos or "Barney."*

The three watched rock videos for half an hour, and then Darcy had to leave. Just as she did, Mrs. Taylor came home from the library. "Hello, girls," she said, putting some books down on the coffee table. "How was your day?"

"Mine was okay," Allie said. "Stephanie's was the pits."

"Oh, no." Mrs. Taylor looked concerned. "And this was the day you worked in the cafeteria, too. What happened?"

"Nothing," Stephanie said. "At least, nothing good. And I was so busy in the cafeteria I didn't have a single second to look for any evidence for my story. I don't know what I'll do if I don't find anything tomorrow."

"Well, there's no sense in worrying about that now," Mrs. Taylor said. "What you need is something to take your mind off it."

"Uh-oh," Allie said to Stephanie. "She's talking about chores."

Remembering her manners, Stephanie said, "I don't mind helping with the chores, Mrs. Taylor." She looked around the spotless living room, but there was absolutely nothing she could do to make it cleaner.

"Well, there's one chore I've been putting off," Mrs. Taylor said, motioning for Allie and Stephanie to follow her into the dining room. "It's a big job, but with three of us doing it, we'll be finished in no time. So you'll be doing me a favor, Stephanie. And if it helps you forget your worries, then that'll be my favor to you."

The "favor" turned out to be polishing the silverware. It didn't look tarnished to Stephanie, but what did she know about sterling silver? And "no time" turned out to be an hour and a half.

"There!" Mrs. Taylor said when they'd finally finished. "We're done and it looks beautiful.

Thank you both. Why don't you just relax now while I fix dinner?"

Which reminds me, Stephanie thought. *I didn't get to finish lunch. No wonder my stomach's been rumbling like a volcano!*

Back in the living room, Allie was just about to turn on the TV again when the phone rang. "I bet it's Darcy," she said, picking it up. "Hi, Darce. Listen, you'll never believe . . . Oh, hi, Mr. Tanner!" She listened for a second, then laughed. "Sure, she's right here." Allie held the phone out to Stephanie. "Your dad asked for Special Undercover Agent Tanner," she whispered.

Still treating it like a joke, Stephanie thought, taking the phone. "Hi, Dad."

"Hi, honey. How did everything go today?"

"Well . . . I learned a lot." This was true. She'd learned how to dish up peaches and potatoes in record-breaking time.

"You mean you uncovered an evil food plot? Just a second, Steph," Danny said. "Michelle, honey, why don't you and the twins play hide-and-seek upstairs?"

In the background Stephanie could hear Michelle counting and one of the twins giggling loudly.

"Michelle?" Danny said again. "Nicky? Never mind. Stephanie?"

"I'm still here, Dad."

"Where were we? Oh, right, you were telling me that you'd discovered something in the cafeteria kitchen."

"Well, no. Not exactly," Stephanie had to admit.

"Oh. Well, today was just your first try.... Nicky, don't get tangled up in the phone cord! Hang on a minute, Stephanie."

There was another pause, and Stephanie heard Michelle yell "twenty!" and Nicky giggle some more. Then the phone was picked up again. This time it was Becky. "Hi, Stephanie. I only have a second—I have to get Nicky out of here—but I just wanted to ask how your story's going."

Of all the people in her family, Becky was the only one who'd treated Stephanie's story seriously. She wished she had something good to report. "Well, it's coming along," was all she could think of to say.

"Great! Sorry, Stephanie, but I've got to go. We miss you. Here's your dad."

"Becky's right, Steph," Danny said. "We miss you. It's so quiet with you not here."

Stephanie had to laugh. "It sounds pretty noisy to me."

"Oh, well, you know what I mean, honey. So. I guess you'll be staying at the Taylors' another night since . . ."

"Yeah," Stephanie said. "I've got to get the story done." *If only I had a story to write.*

"Well . . . okay. I wish . . . oops, gotta go, Stephanie! Alex just came in and decided to hide under Comet. Bye, sweetheart. Love you."

"Bye, Dad. Love you, too." Stephanie hung up.

"What's happening at home?" Allie asked.

"The usual," Stephanie said with a laugh. "Total chaos."

After dinner Allie and Stephanie did some homework together. Then Stephanie flopped down on her bed in the attic. She was exhausted from feeding five-hundred starving students and polishing sterling silver for twelve. But she forced herself to get up.

At the desk she took out the outline for her newspaper story and stared at it. But there was absolutely nothing more she could add to it.

What was she going to do?

Don't start feeling sorry for yourself, Stephanie

thought. *Go talk to Allie. Go have a snack and watch some television. You'll come up with some evidence tomorrow.*

Allie was working on an English paper, so Stephanie joined Mr. and Mrs. Taylor in the living room. They were eating apples and watching a program on soldier ants. Stephanie was dying for a Twinkie, but she ate an apple. And she watched a little of the program, but after five minutes she was totally bored. On the excitement scale, soldier ants ranked right down there with watching the grass grow.

Too bad Michelle can't come in and switch the station to "Looney Tunes," she thought.

Stephanie stayed long enough to finish her apple, then said good night. Allie was still busy with her paper, and Stephanie couldn't think of anything else to do. *You wouldn't have that problem at home,* she thought. *But you wouldn't be able to write your story, either.*

Back in the attic she spent a little time fooling with her hair, trying to get it ready for tomorrow's hair net. But it was a lost cause. Finally she gave up and went to bed.

She thought she'd fall asleep in seconds. Instead, she lay there with her eyes wide open and her ears straining for something, *any*thing to break the silence. Amazed, she found herself wishing Michelle were there, chatting to her stuffed animals, or that the twins would race in giggling and squealing.

Totally incredible! she thought. *I actually miss the noise!* Telling herself she'd be home as soon as she got her story done, Stephanie closed her eyes and started counting sheep.

CHAPTER
9

◆ ◀ ▪ ◆

"All right, Tanner!" McDougal barked. "Today's special is sloppy joes. Rosie'll get the buns on the trays, you fill 'em up." She handed Stephanie a ladle and pointed to an enormous pot filled with the sloppy-joe mixture.

Stephanie adjusted her hair net and pulled on her Baggies. Day two of the lunch lady from Mars had begun.

"After you do the joes, get the chocolate cupcakes from the freezer, six boxes, and microwave them for two minutes on high, about ten at a time," McDougal ordered. Then she turned to her second-in-command. "Rosie, don't forget the salad dressing. Oh, and check the hamburger buns. A couple of days ago I found a whole loaf of bread that was moldy."

Stephanie's ears perked up when she heard the word *moldy*. *Maybe Sergeant McDougal would tell Rosie just to pick the moldy parts off,* Stephanie thought. *Or to go ahead and use the buns if the mold hadn't turned green yet. Maybe I'm finally going to get my scoop!*

"I called the bakery and chewed them out." McDougal chuckled. "I'm pretty sure it won't happen again. But just make sure, Rosie."

So much for the moldy bread theory. Disappointed, Stephanie picked up the ladle and stirred the goopy meat mixture. *Now what? She had to find something. This was her last chance!*

McDougal headed for the door. "Okay, ladies, get to work. I'll be back in ten minutes."

Did she say ten minutes? Stephanie smiled. As soon as Mrs. McDougal left the kitchen, she went into action, filling hamburger buns with meat and making the cupcakes as quickly as she could. Then she started searching for clues. If it wasn't going to be moldy bread, then it would have to be something else, like bugs or labels that said things like "Good until April 12, 1903"

97

or "Danger, poison." She checked out both microwaves, inside and out. In the refrigerator she looked for milk cartons with overdue dates. The rest of the staff was too busy to notice Stephanie sneaking around.

By the time McDougal returned and sent her out onto the serving line, Stephanie had combed the whole kitchen, from top to bottom.

"So? What did you find?" an excited Darcy asked as she and Allie joined Stephanie in the girls' bathroom after lunch. "The milk was sour, right?"

"Nope."

"The sloppy joes had ants in them?" Allie said hopefully.

"I found nothing. Zilch. Zero," Stephanie said, frustrated. "Now help me get this fishnet off my head so I can look like a human being again."

"Not until I take a picture," Darcy said, whipping out an instant camera from her book bag.

"No way!" Stephanie tried to yank the hair net off, but it was tangled again. "How could you possibly think I'd want my picture taken when I look like this?"

"You never know," Darcy said. "It might come in handy."

"For what? Blackmailers?"

"No. For your story. Maybe it'll give you some inspiration. Come on," Darcy insisted. "Say . . . 'meat loaf!' "

Before Stephanie could stop her, Darcy snapped the picture. As the photograph came out of the camera, the three friends gathered around to check it out.

"The only thing this picture makes me want to do is crawl into the biggest hole I can find." Stephanie groaned. "Now let me have it so I can destroy it."

"But I wanted to send it off to 'America's Most Wanted,' " Darcy kidded. " 'Beware! This girl may be impersonating a lunch lady in *your* cafeteria!' "

"Hand it over."

Darcy gave the snapshot to Stephanie.

"And let me have the negatives."

"There are no negatives," Darcy explained. "It's an instant camera. Anyway, you know I'd never try to blackmail you, Steph. Go ahead and rip it up if you want to."

Stephanie looked at the picture again. "Maybe

I won't," she said, slipping the photograph into the pocket of her orange miniskirt. "Maybe I'll keep it to remind me of my brief but undistinguished career as an ace investigative reporter for *The Scribe.*"

"Steph! You're not giving up, are you?" Allie asked.

"Why not? I don't have a story, remember?"

"Well, maybe you don't have a super-exposé, but you can think of *some*thing to write," Darcy said. "Besides, if you give up, you'll never make the paper. And you would have dressed up like a lunch lady from Mars for nothing!"

"You're right." Stephanie yanked the hair net off her head and started combing her hair. "The old Stephanie might have quit. But the new Stephanie's going to keep trying. Thanks for reminding me, guys."

Later that afternoon, just as Stephanie and Allie met up at their lockers, a flash of lightning lit up the hallway.

Allie groaned. "Rain again? I'm telling you, Steph, it's a curse to have hair that frizzes."

A thunderbolt shook the air, and a heavy rain began to fall outside.

"See. I told you. I *am* cursed!" Allie said, stuffing some books in her locker. "I didn't even bring an umbrella."

"Relax. I've got one." Reaching into her own locker, Stephanie pulled out Michelle's umbrella, which she'd stashed after using it the day before to avoid Brandon.

"I thought you hated being seen with that thing."

"That was before I started working in the cafeteria," Stephanie said. "After being seen in a hair net, carrying a duck umbrella doesn't faze me at all. Come on, let's go before we miss the bus."

As the girls joined the bus line, Stephanie saw that two Flamingoes, Tiffany and Tara, were also in line, and that they were checking out the duck umbrella. Stephanie prepared herself for a nasty comment, but the Flamingoes didn't say a word. They just looked at each other and shrugged.

"What do you suppose is wrong with them?" Stephanie whispered to Allie. "They're not making any snide remarks about the umbrella. I'm almost disappointed."

Allie giggled. "Maybe they've run out of snide remarks."

"Never," Stephanie said. "Oh, well, at least that's one good thing to happen today."

Back in the Taylors' quiet house, which was even quieter than usual because the television was on the blink, Stephanie and Allie stretched out on the living room floor and played cards.

"Three of hearts. I win." Allie laid her hand down on the rug. "That's ten straight, Steph. What's going on? I never win when we play cards."

"I know! I don't get it, either." Stephanie tossed her hand down. "I guess I'm just not concentrating." She looked around the immaculate living room. "Hey, why don't we play the piano? If we can't have a rock video, at least we can have music."

But "Chopsticks" got boring after a while, and soon Stephanie retired to her room to tackle her cafeteria story. She cleared the desk and put a blank piece of paper in front of her.

Okay. What do I have to expose? Not the moldy bread, that's for sure. But there's no question the kitchen is understaffed. Yawn! And the refrigerators could use some updating. B-o-r-i-n-g!

An hour later, her pencil well-chewed and the

102

paper still blank, Stephanie's mind began to wander. She wondered if her dad had made sure all the cereal boxes were lined up alphabetically in the kitchen cabinet. If Nicky had learned to keep his pants on. And if Michelle had turned Stephanie's side of the room into a menagerie with all her stuffed animals.

"I'll bet you've already written a whole book," Allie said, stepping into the attic.

"Not even a postcard," Stephanie said, holding up the blank sheet of paper. "It doesn't look like Stephanie Tanner, ace reporter, is going to write the story of the century today. Maybe not even this year."

"The creative juices aren't flowing, huh?"

"They aren't even dripping!"

"My mom says dinner will be ready soon. We could go down and polish silver again!"

"No, it's my brain that needs polishing. I just can't think!"

Allie sat down on the bed. "Look. It's Friday, and you've got the whole weekend to work on it. If it's not raining, why don't we play tennis tomorrow morning? Just you, me, and Darcy. Then, tomorrow afternoon you can come back here and work on your story for the rest of the day."

Stephanie had almost forgotten that it was Friday. Just three days left before she had to turn in the story. But Allie's suggestion made sense. "Why not?" Stephanie said. "Right now all I'm doing is spinning my wheels."

"Great!"

"But I'll have to go home and get my tennis racket." Stephanie crumbled up the blank sheet of paper and grabbed Michelle's umbrella. "Be back in about ten minutes, Allie."

CHAPTER
10

♦ ◀ ♦ ♦

The minute Stephanie opened the front door of her house, Nicky dashed by in his underpants and raced up the stairs. Stephanie grinned. That much was the same, anyway.

First things first, she told herself, putting the dripping duck umbrella in the stand by the front door. *Twinkies.* She was taking one of the spongy little cakes from the cupboard when Jesse walked in.

"Well, hi, stranger," he said.

"Hi, Uncle Jesse."

"Are you back to stay?"

"No, just to get my tennis racket," Stephanie told him. "And some junk food."

"Don't eat it yet. You're just in time for the remains of another fabulous dinner," Jesse said. "Sit. It'll only take a second to warm up."

Obviously aware that food was about to be served, Comet trotted into the room, followed by Danny. When Danny saw Stephanie, he stopped, surprised. "Stephanie, you're home!"

"Just to get her tennis racket," Jesse said, turning on the oven.

Taking the Twinkie with her, Stephanie sat down at the table. "Allie, Darcy, and I are going to play tomorrow morning," she explained.

"Oh." Danny looked disappointed. "I was sort of hoping you were back to stay."

"Yeah, well. The story's not done yet."

"My umbrella's back!" Michelle shouted as she entered the kitchen, carrying the umbrella. "I thought I'd never see it again."

"It's all yours, Michelle," Stephanie said. "And thanks. It got me out of a few tight spots."

Michelle popped the umbrella open and twirled it around, spraying everybody with raindrops.

"Here you are, Stephanie," Jesse announced,

putting a plate on the table. "Twice-cooked pep-peroni pizza." Stephanie wolfed it down, then reached for the Twinkie.

"Didn't they feed you at Allie's house?" Danny asked, sounding concerned.

"Uh-huh, but I'm still hungry."

"I didn't know we had Twinkies," Michelle said.

"That's because Dad hides them." Stephanie broke off a piece of the cake and gave it to her sister. "But I know where to look."

"Drats," Danny said. "Foiled again."

Becky came into the kitchen with the twins, both fully dressed. "Stephanie, hi!"

"Hi, Becky."

Becky turned to Jesse. "I thought you were going to get Nicky's pants on him."

"I was, but he hid from me."

Becky laughed and gave Stephanie a hug. "It's great to have you back, Steph!"

"Steph-nie back. Steph-nie back," Alex said cheerfully.

"How's the story going?" Becky asked.

"Yeah. Find anymore incriminating evidence in the cafeteria kitchen?" Jesse asked. "A cock-roach the size of a shoebox, maybe?"

"To tell you the truth, I have less now than when I started," Stephanie admitted.

"Hmm. So how *are* you going to write the story?" Danny asked.

"I don't know," Stephanie moaned. "And I have to turn it in on Monday."

Jesse looked at Comet. "It's all your fault, Comet. Bad dog."

"Bad dog," Nicky echoed.

Comet lay down on the floor and gave out a pathetic whine. Everyone laughed. Then Becky nudged Jesse, and Danny put his finger on his lips and frowned at Michelle and the twins. The laughter stopped suddenly. The grown-ups exchanged glances and looked embarrassed. "Sorry, Steph," Jesse apologized. "I know you're serious about that story. I shouldn't have made a joke."

There was an uncomfortable moment of silence.

Stephanie shook her head. "Listen, guys. It's not Comet's fault and I'm sorry I lost my temper the other day because it's not your fault, either. As for my story, I'll work it out." She reached into her skirt pocket and held out the snapshot Darcy had taken. "You don't think I'd get dressed up like this for nothing, do you?"

Everyone crowded around to look at the picture.

"Spaceman?" Alex said.

"That's right, Alex. It's the lunch lady from outer space." Stephanie sighed and got up from the kitchen table. "Well, I'd better go up and get my tennis racket."

"Please don't ruin the tent," Michelle pleaded.

"Don't worry, I'm not staying," Stephanie reminded her, not quite knowing what to expect in her room.

The "tent" was Stephanie's bed, her blanket propped up with her tennis racket, and all Michelle's stuffed animals neatly tucked inside it like furry little campers. Stephanie was trying to figure out how to take her racket without collapsing the tent when D.J. rushed into the room. "Am I glad you're back!"

"Thanks, D.J." Stephanie paused. "You are?"

"Sure! I mean, Steph, with you gone, Michelle's been driving *me* bonkers."

Stephanie laughed. "Sorry about that. But I'm not staying. I just came for my tennis racket." She pointed to the tent.

"Isn't there anything I can say to change your mind?"

Stephanie shook her head.

Looking disappointed, D.J. left. About ten seconds later Joey came in.

"Hey, Stephanie, I heard you were back," he said. "Look, I don't want to be the one to say I told you so, but, I told you so. If you'd listened to me, you could have broken the hottest story since E.T."

"Come on, Joey. You don't really believe aliens landed in New Mexico?"

"Well, no. But I'm sure you could have given it the right spin to make it sound real. Anyway, I just wanted to say I've missed you and it's good to have you back."

Before Stephanie could tell Joey she wasn't staying, he left and Michelle came in. She stopped in the middle of the room and cleared her throat. "Thank you for returning my umbrella, and I hope you don't go," she said, turning around and leaving again.

Something weird is going on, Stephanie thought.

Next in the parade of family members were the twins.

"Steph-nie stay?" the boys said in chorus.

"Let me guess," Stephanie said. "You missed me, didn't you?"

Both boys nodded.

Stephanie thought for a moment. "Listen, guys. Did somebody tell you to come up here and ask me to stay?"

The boys nodded again and then ran over to Michelle's "tent" and started playing with the stuffed animals.

I thought so, Stephanie said to herself. *And I bet I know who.*

Next in line was Comet, who sat down in the doorway.

"Okay, Comet. What do you have to say?"

Comet barked.

"Yeah, well. You know I should be really mad at you for eating my evidence that turned out not to be evidence."

Comet barked again, wagging his tail, but still not entering the room.

"Okay, boy, I forgive you. Come here."

When Comet dashed over to Stephanie, she bent down to hug him, and he started licking her face.

"It looks as if you and Comet have made peace with each other," Danny said from the doorway. "Alex, Nicky, why don't you take Comet downstairs? I need to talk to Stephanie alone."

Comet barked and followed the twins, almost knocking them over on the way out. Danny made a small place for himself on Stephanie's bed and sat down.

"So, Steph. It's been a long time. I hardly recognize you. You're so . . . grown-up."

"Come on, Dad. I'm on to your campaign to get me to stay."

"Campaign?" Danny tried to look innocent. "What campaign?"

"D.J. and Joey were pretty good, but you should never have sent Michelle."

"Okay, I admit it. But I miss you, honey. We all do. I wish you wouldn't leave again."

"I've missed you, too."

"Oh, yeah? What did you miss the most?" Danny asked.

Stephanie thought for a moment. "The way you arrange all our dairy products by cholesterol count."

"Doesn't everybody do that?"

"No, I mean it," Stephanie said. "I guess I'm just used to the craziness around here. Allie's house is nice and everything. But it's so quiet! This place is more like a zoo."

On cue, Comet let out a long steady howl

that was followed by the twins trying to dupli-
cate it.

"Definitely a zoo." Danny nodded. "I guess
quiet's better for your story, though, so you'll be
going back to Allie's tonight to work on it."

"Dad. The story's a non-story."

"Really having trouble, huh?" Danny said. "I
have a suggestion. Maybe you should try writing
the story from a different angle."

"What other angle could there be? The meat
loaf's point of view?"

"Now that you mention it, why not? 'My Life
As a Meat Loaf Sandwich, by Stephanie Tanner.' "

Stephanie laughed.

"See?" Danny said. "One of the special things
about you is that you can usually find the humor
in a situation."

"Yeah. I sure haven't been laughing very
much lately, though."

"Well, I think you've been trying to change things
that don't need changing," Danny said gently.

"Dad, I have a confession to make."

"What is it, Steph?"

Stephanie pushed a few stuffed animals aside
and sat down next to her father. "I *really* miss
being home."

"You do?"

"Yes, and your campaign worked. I'm staying."

Danny gave Stephanie a big hug. "Welcome back."

Just then Jesse entered the room. "Hi, Steph. Just wanted to come by and say . . ."

Danny grabbed Jesse before he could finish his sentence and escorted him out. After a minute Stephanie followed and went to the living room to call Allie.

"What are you doing?" Allie said. "I thought you'd be right back."

"I did, too. But I've decided to move back home," Stephanie said. "I can't explain exactly why. I mean, I love your house and it was great of you to let me come stay, but . . . I don't know. I guess I belong here. Do you understand?"

"Sure," Allie said. "And listen, if you ever need to escape again, you know where we live. But what about tomorrow morning? Are we still on for tennis?"

"Absolutely, if I can figure out how to get my racket back. See you tomorrow."

Stephanie went back to her room, feeling good. She pushed a few more stuffed animals aside and crawled into the tent. Upstairs, the twins were singing along with Becky. Comet was barking in the kitchen, and Michelle and Joey were horsing around on the living room couch. It was loud. It was crazy. It was . . . normal!

Stephanie reached into her pocket and pulled out the photo of the "Lunch Lady." In spite of herself, she giggled. *Here she is,* Stephanie thought, *the brand-new me. It wasn't exactly what I had in mind when I started seventh grade and wanted to make big changes in myself.*

Maybe I would have been better off if I'd followed Joey's suggestion and written about space aliens.

Suddenly something clicked in her head—a way to write the cafeteria story.

"Yes!" she said out loud. Popping out of the tent, she sat down at her desk, grabbed a sheet of paper, and feverishly began to write.

CHAPTER
11

◆ ◀ ◆ ◆

"Let me see if I've got this straight," Allie said. "You're going to write about aliens landing in New Mexico?"

Stephanie shook her head. "No, I'm going to write about cafeteria food."

"So what's with the aliens?" Darcy asked. "Are they going to take meat loaf samples back to their home planet?"

It was a bright, sunny morning for a change. The girls were decked out in sweatsuits, Stephanie in yellow, Allie in blue, Darcy in red. Each had a tennis racket, and Darcy was also carrying a can of balls. They were walking to the public tennis courts a few blocks away, and Stephanie was trying to explain to her friends how she'd gotten the inspiration for her story.

"It was something Joey said about the aliens," Stephanie told them. "He said I could write a believable story. But I couldn't—not without any facts. And that's what the cafeteria story is missing. Facts."

The girls reached the tennis courts, opened a tall wire door, and walked onto the playing area. Two courts were taken, one by an elderly couple and the other by two very cute guys. The last court was free. They tossed their jackets down and began to warm up.

"But it's more than just not having any facts," Stephanie continued as she swung her racket back and forth in the air. "Look at me. Do I look like a cutthroat investigative reporter?"

"Is this a trick question?" Allie asked, reaching down and touching her toes.

"No."

"I don't know. I never met one."

"Use your imagination," Stephanie suggested, tightening her sneaker laces.

"You don't look like a cutthroat investigative reporter to me," Darcy said as she jogged in place, then did deep-knee bends.

"That's right. And I'm not. The problem is, I tried to be one."

Darcy trotted to the net. "Yeah, I guess I understand," she called back. Then she jumped over the net and walked to the far end of the court.

"I guess I do, too." Allie began to bounce a tennis ball on her racket. "But what are you going to write?"

Stephanie just smiled. "I'll read it to you on Monday, and then you'll see. Come on, let's play!"

Since Darcy was much better at tennis than Stephanie and Allie, she played against them. Although Stephanie's "team" lost most of the games, she had a lot of fun. And all the girls had even more fun when the ball went onto the court next to them—where the two cute guys were playing.

After the girls finished playing, they stopped off for ice cream. Then Stephanie bought a box of candy and went to Allie's house, where she gave it to Mrs. Taylor as a thank-you.

"It was our pleasure," Mrs. Taylor said warmly.

After that Stephanie went straight home to begin writing.

In spite of the constant interruptions, Stephanie worked all afternoon on her story. When her fingers were about to fall off, she took a break. Lying on her bed, she thought about the *new* Stephanie. On a scale of one to ten, she rated a minus five! So, she decided to discuss the situation with the only one in the house who would listen to her without interrupting.

"See, it's like this," Stephanie explained. "The *new* Stephanie has some positives, like wanting to get to school on time and paying attention in class."

Comet was all ears. He sat on the carpet in Stephanie's room, wagging his tail and grinning at her.

"But she also has some negatives," Stephanie continued. "Like being too serious about everything and not having any fun. Maybe she's trying to be someone she's not. So I've decided that what the *new* Stephanie needs is some of the *old* Stephanie back. Sort of like a *new new-old* Stephanie. Get it?"

119

Comet yawned.

"Never mind. Get out of here. Go find a moldy piece of bread to eat."

Comet left, and as Stephanie sat down to write the final paragraphs of her story, there was one more interruption.

"Steph! You gotta do me a favor," D.J. said as she walked into the room. Michelle slipped in right after her. "Remember Charlie Reese? Well, he got two tickets to the rock concert tonight."

"That's cool, D.J." Stephanie looked up from her story. "When do we leave?"

Michelle giggled.

"Don't take this personally, Steph, but I thought Charlie and I would go to the concert, and you and I would swap dishwashing days. After all, you got out of your chores while you were gone, remember? What do you say?"

"How could I resist an offer like that, D.J.?"

"She can't do it," Michelle announced, standing in front of Stephanie's to-do list. "It says right here that Stephanie's dishwashing day is tomorrow."

"That's right, it does, Michelle." Stephanie got up and went to the list. "But sometimes you have to be flexible." Stephanie took her pencil and crossed out her Sunday dishwashing duty and wrote it in on Saturday.

"Is that allowed?" Michelle asked.

"Sure. It's *my* to-do list. I made it up and I can change it if I want to."

"Hey, thanks, Steph," D.J. said. "I've got to go get ready. See you at dinner."

Michelle stayed behind. "I thought this list was important."

"It is. But other things are important, too." Pointing to Michelle's smiling sun, which Stephanie had taped up next to the list, she went on. "When I tried to be so super-organized, I wasn't having very many nice days."

Michelle thought a minute. "Does this mean you're going to be the old Stephanie again?"

Stephanie grinned. "Let's just call it the *real* Stephanie."

"No lie, Steph, it's a great story," Allie said.

"Better than great," Darcy added. "It's awesome!"

It was Monday morning—the day Stephanie had to turn in her story. Despite a weekend of laughing and crying twins, a howling dog, and

121

sisters barging into her room, she managed to write it. She'd let Allie and Darcy read it on the school bus, and they loved the story.

But they would have probably liked anything I wrote, Stephanie thought to herself. She was beginning to have some doubts as they walked down the hallway to *The Scribe* office.

"Hi, guys," Sue called out as she caught up to the threesome. "That your story?" she asked, pointing to the paper in Stephanie's hand.

"This is it." Stephanie glanced down at her paper. The upper-left corner was chewed up—Comet's contribution.

"Well, I've got mine, too." Sue held up a few sheets of neatly typed paragraphs.

"What's it about? Darcy asked.

"Soldier ants."

"Soldier ants?" Stephanie said. "Did you watch that boring show, too?"

"Uh-huh. It was awful, but when I found out that Billy Klepper got straight A's in science, I thought I'd write a nature piece."

"Come on, girls," Mrs. Blith called out from her desk inside the office. "If you've got a story, turn it in now, or you'll be late for your first class."

Sue walked into the office and dropped her story on Mrs. Blith's desk. Stephanie hesitated.

"Go on!" Darcy prompted her.

Stephanie took a deep breath, then placed her story on Mrs. Blith's desk.

"I can't believe it," Stephanie said nervously to Allie and Darcy as the three girls headed off to their first class. "Mrs. Blith said she'd call the winners at home later today."

"So?" Darcy adjusted the shoulder strap on her book bag.

"So. That's like a hundred years from now," Stephanie complained. "What am I going to do until then?"

"Chew a lot of pencils," Darcy suggested.

About six hours and five chewed pencils later, the three girls were at their lockers getting ready to leave school.

Get a grip, Tanner, Stephanie said to herself as all her stuff fell out of her book bag.

Allie and Darcy helped her retrieve the pencils, gum, barrettes, change, and a million other things and shove them back into her bag.

"Calm down, Steph. You're losing it," Darcy said.

"Losing what?" Stephanie said, picking up her bus pass. "My mind? My will to live? My future career as a writer? I'm going nuts, guys," Stephanie continued. "You have to come home with me. Just don't let me wait this thing out alone."

"Hey, what are friends for?" Darcy said. "We'll even chew some pencils with you."

"Thanks." After she'd gathered up all her things, Stephanie picked out the books she'd need for the night's homework—although she couldn't imagine how she'd get anything done until the phone call came.

But what if it doesn't come? Stephanie thought a moment later. *Then what? I'll never make it as a writer. I'll probably spend my whole life as a lunch lady.*

"Stephanie," a voice called out from behind her—breaking into her gloomy thoughts. It was Brandon Fallow. "Hi, Darce, Allie."

"Hi, Brandon," the girls replied.

"Listen. Stephanie. I have a question for you," Brandon said.

Stephanie wasn't sure she was in any condition to answer questions—even from Brandon Fallow. "Sure, Brandon. What?" she asked, trying to keep her cool.

"That *was* you I saw with a duck umbrella the other day, wasn't it?"

Uh oh, Stephanie thought to herself. *He recognized me!* "You mean the one with the *yellow* ducks?" she said, stalling for time to come up with a better answer.

"Yeah, that's the one." Brandon smiled. "I don't know why Jenni was laughing at it. I told her I thought it was pretty cool."

"Yeah, well, see it's not really mine. I mean, under normal circumstances, I wouldn't be caught ..." Stephanie stopped. "Wait a minute. Did you say you thought the duck umbrella was ..."

"Cool," Darcy finished, giving Stephanie a nudge. "He said he thought it was cool, Steph."

"Right." Brandon smiled again. "Catch you later."

"You're blushing, Stephanie," Allie said after Brandon had left.

"I know, but at least I'm not giggling." Stephanie shook her head. "Wait'll the shock wears off. *Then* I'll giggle."

A few minutes later, as the three friends walked out into a light rain to catch the school bus, Stephanie came to a complete standstill and pointed to the bus line.

Standing in line were three Flamingoes—Jenni, Tara, and Tiffany. And above each Flamingo's head was an umbrella—an umbrella with little ducks printed on it. The ducks were pink, but they were definitely ducks.

Stepping up to Tiffany, Stephanie pointed to the umbrella.

"Cool," she said with a satisfied smile.

CHAPTER
12

♦ ◀ ▸ ♦

As soon as Stephanie got home, she plopped herself down on the couch in the living room and stared at the telephone on the coffee table. Allie and Darcy sat down next to her. The house was unusually quiet. Then Michelle came into the living room.

"Hi, you guys," she said turning on the TV. "You want to watch 'Looney Tunes'?"

"Do we have to?" Darcy said, half kidding.

"Uh-huh." Michelle squeezed herself onto the couch, in between Stephanie and Darcy. "Oh, I almost forgot to tell you," she said to her sister without taking her eyes off the TV.

Full House: Stephanie

"Tell me what, Michelle," Stephanie asked, not taking *her* eyes off the phone.

"You got a phone call."

"A phone call?" Stephanie leaped off the couch. "A phone call? From who?"

"Somebody from school," Michelle said. "I *think* her name was Bright."

"Blith? You mean Blith?" Stephanie asked excitedly.

"Maybe," Michelle answered.

"Are you going to tell us what she said?" Darcy asked.

"Well. Let me think." Michelle put her finger to her chin. "I can't remember exactly."

Stephanie grabbed her sister by the shoulders. "Think, Michelle. Think. Did she say I made it? Did she say I'm on *The Scribe?*"

All of a sudden the whole Tanner extended family came marching down the stairs. Danny, Joey, and Jesse were tooting party favors left over from last New Year's. The twins were beating their toy drums. Comet was barking.

"You made it! You made it!" Danny yelled out as the group encircled Stephanie around the couch. Danny gave his daughter a big hug.

"I made it?" Stephanie said. "I really made it?"

"Mrs. Blith called about a half hour ago and said you turned in one of the best stories," Becky said as she hugged Stephanie. Everyone exchanged high fives. The twins kept beating their drums, and Comet let out a loud howl.

"So, Steph," D.J. called out over the commotion. "How much longer are you going to keep us in suspense?"

"Yeah, read us your story," Jesse followed.

"Go ahead." Allie nudged Stephanie. "They'll love it."

"Well, all right," Stephanie said, a little embarrassed as she pulled two pieces of paper out of her book bag.

"Quiet, everybody. Quiet!" Danny yelled. "Introducing ace reporter for *The Scribe*, Miss Stephanie Tanner."

Everyone applauded. Stephanie faced the group. "Thanks, Dad." She smoothed out her paper, cleared her throat, and began to read.

"The Meat Loaf Caper, *by Stephanie Tanner.*
"Tanner's my name and cafeteria crime's my game. It's a dirty job, but somebody's got to do it. And the message on my answering machine

sounded desperate: 'Help. Meat loaf running wild in school cafeteria. Come quick.'

"I had many questions. Was the meat loaf cooked? Was it marinated? Was it dangerous? The last thought stuck in my throat. But an ace crime-fighter doesn't choke. There was only one way to get my answers: Follow the meat loaf.

"The job called for undercover work, so I put on my fishnet, a pair of forty-nine-cent plastic Baggies with fingers, and a white apron, five sizes too large. I looked like the lunch lady from Mars. It was the perfect disguise.

"What I found at the scene of the crime wasn't a pretty sight. Sure, there was a meat loaf running wild. But could you blame him with five hundred angry students carrying 'Down with Meat Loaf' signs, chasing him around the room?

"This is a meat loaf who, day after day, listens to cruel jokes and wisecracks about his appearance; a meat loaf who often spends the last moments of his life at the bottom of a trash can. And why? Because he's one tough piece of meat, no matter what the cafeteria crew tries to do to him. True, he's no chicken parm. And his brownish green glow isn't very appetizing. But is that any reason to make him an endangered species?

"I explained all this to the angry students. You don't have to eat him, I told them. Just give him some respect. After a few tense moments the students gave in and let the meat loaf go.

"Despite this unfortunate incident at the John Muir Middle School, cafeteria officials there continue to list meat loaf on the menu. Some things never change. Some things never should. The End."

Stephanie barely had time to look up before she was showered with applause and whistles.

"Bravo!" Joey yelled out. "Author! Author!"

The twins, not really knowing what was going on, joined in the clapping.

Danny had a big smile on his face. "Wasn't that the greatest thing you've ever heard?"

"That *was* terrific, Steph!" Becky said. "It sounded just like you."

Yeah, Stephanie thought, *the real me*.

"Pretty funny stuff, Steph." D.J. grinned. "I loved the part about the chicken parm."

"Wasn't that the greatest thing you've ever heard?" Danny said again, smiling around the table.

131

The only one who didn't join in the praise was Michelle. She sat there quietly until Danny finally noticed her. "What's wrong, honey?" he asked. "Wasn't that the greatest thing you ever heard?"

"It was the *saddest* thing I ever heard," Michelle said, trying to hold back her tears. "That poor meat loaf!"

"Don't take it so hard," Stephanie told her sister. "It was only a story. And by the way. I owe you a thank-you."

"You do?" Michelle asked.

"Yes," Stephanie said, sitting down on the couch next to her sister. "Thanks to you, duck umbrellas have become a major fashion statement at school."

She explained about the Flamingoes and their new umbrellas. "So I was wondering—you don't happen to have any more funky umbrellas stashed away in your closet, do you? See, now that I've become a trendsetter, I have to stay one step ahead of the competition."

"I've got one with frogs sitting on lily pads," Michelle said.

"Frogs on lily pads? I like it." Stephanie laughed. "What do you think, Darce?"

"Sounds cool to me."

"And by the time the Flamingoes find pink frogs," Allie added, "you can switch umbrellas on them again!"

"Stephanie," Joey called out. "I've got something for you. It's a special gift for making *The Scribe.*" He pulled a small, tissue-wrapped package out of his shirt pocket and handed it to her.

"What is it?" Allie asked.

"Go ahead. Open it and find out," Joey said.

Stephanie unwrapped the package and pulled out a pair of Groucho Marx glasses with a rubber nose and a bristly black mustache attached to them.

"I thought they'd come in handy for your next undercover job," Joey said.

"Thanks, Joey." Stephanie put the glasses on.

After the laughter died down, D.J. had a question for her sister. "Steph. I don't get something. Didn't you say you were going to write a super-serious story? What made you change your mind?"

"It's kind of hard to explain," Stephanie said, adjusting her Groucho glasses. "But I finally realized that 'super-serious' just isn't me. Like being totally organized just isn't me, either. I guess I was trying to change my whole personality and it wasn't working. I mean, I'm still going to try to be more organized and responsible and stuff, like I told Comet, but—"

"Like you told *Comet?*" D.J. interrupted. "You discussed this with the dog?"

"Sure. He's a great listener." Stephanie reached down and petted Comet. "Anyway, once I figured out that I was trying to be somebody I wasn't, I knew I couldn't write a story that wasn't me, either."

"Well, it sounds as if you and Comet worked it out perfectly," Danny said.

"You helped, too, Dad," Stephanie told him. "Your idea about 'Life As a Meat Loaf Sandwich' really got me thinking."

"So, Steph," Becky asked. "Got any ideas for your next article?"

"You know, I think I do," Stephanie said. "Maybe I'll do a story about family life. *This* family's life."

"Well, that should certainly be fascinating," Danny said. "What will you call it?"

Stephanie pushed the Groucho glasses up on her nose and looked around. "How about, 'Inside the San Francisco Zoo'?"

134

A series of novels based on your favorite
character from the hit TV show!

FULL HOUSE™
Stephanie

PHONE CALL FROM A FLAMINGO

THE BOY-OH-BOY NEXT DOOR

TWIN TROUBLES

HIP HOP TILL YOU DROP

HERE COMES THE BRAND NEW ME

THE SECRET'S OUT

DADDY'S NOT-SO-LITTLE GIRL

P.S. FRIENDS FOREVER

GETTING EVEN WITH THE FLAMINGOES

THE DUDE OF MY DREAMS

Available from Minstrel® Books
Published by Pocket Books